Blessed
NOT STESSED

Also by Isaiah David Paul

Gritty Faith Fiction
Blessed Not Stressed
King of Kings
Street Disciples
Broken But I'm Healed
Closing My Legs
Try A Little Tenderness (w/Allyson M. Deese)
Ain't Worried About Nothin'
Style & Grayce

Urban/Street Lit/Suspense
I Get Around
KING
Definition of a Bad Girl (writing as MiChaune)

Anthologies
Weary & Will Edited by Sherryle Kiser Jackson
The Triumph of My Soul Edited by Elissa Gabrielle
Soul of a Man Edited by Elissa Gabrielle
Soul of a Man II: Makes Me Wanna Holler by Elissa Gabrielle

Young Adult – Ages 14 & Up
Worth Fighting 4
Boyz 4 Life
U Can't Break Me
R U That Somebody (formerly *Age Ain't Nothing But a Number*)
Never Too Much
Man In The Mirror
Still Standing

Blessed
NOT STESSED

Isaiah David Paul

10's Lee Phelps

www.writesingwork.com
a literary entertainment company

▫Winston-Salem ▪ Denver ▪ Atlanta ▫

Previously published by Abednego's Free as *He Changed My Name* by Jay Imes on October 2006
As *He Changed the Game* by Jarold Imes on February 2009
As *Love Him Like I Do* by Isaiah David Paul on January 2012

10'sLee Phelps & Write Sing Work titles are published by
Write Sing Work, LLC, 6255 Towncenter Drive #1669, Clemmons, North Carolina 27012

Book Credits
Author: Isaiah David Paul
Editors: Tiffany S. Jones, Zee Elle Mae, Kelli Gary & Bethany Hamilton Freebird
Associate Editors: Kiera Drewery Davis and Renee Allen McCoy
Publicity: Kia D. Smith
Model: Nelson J. Davis
Photographer: Anwar "Vdot" Sims

15 14 13 12 11 10 9 8 7 6

Scripture taken from the New King James Version. Copyright © 1982 by Thomas Nelson, Inc. Used by permission. All rights reserved.

Scripture also taken from the Revised Standard Version of the Bible, copyright 1952 [2nd edition, 1971] by the Division of Christian Education of the National Council of the Churches of Christ in the United States of America. Used by permission. All rights reserved.

ISBN 13: 978-1-934195-22-2/ISBN 10: 1-934195-22-7 (print)
ISBN 13: 978-1-934195-56-7/ISBN 10: 1-934195-56-1 (eBook)

The model or models and/or image or images on the cover is a visualization of the story and are not intended to portray any characters or localizations in the book. The photographer and/or models were solicited and compensated for their participation.

Printed in the United States of America & Canada

In Memory of

Kia D. Smith
It's time to make your dreams come true…

Phoebe Medline
Thank you for giving the original version of this
book a chance to breathe

Betty T. Imes
I'm glad you got to see the original version of
this book before you moved on to Glory.

Some things to know before we get started...

for all have sinned and fall short of the glory of God,

Romans 3:23

that if you confess with your mouth the Lord Jesus and believe in your heart that God has raised Him from the dead, you will be saved.

Romans 10:9

Jesus said to him, "'You shall love the LORD your God with all your heart, with all your soul, and with all your mind.' This is the first and great commandment. And the second is like it: 'You shall love your neighbor as yourself.' On these two commandments hang all the Law and the Prophets."

Matthew 22:37-40

Aye Readers,

First, I want to thank you all for standing by me and supporting me as I embark on a new journey. Change is never easy, but sometimes, it's what must be done to go forward.

Without going into details—I obtained the rights back to the Isaiah David Paul name, along with certain intellectual and social media properties. I'm now moving forward with a new purpose for my faith-driven work. For this book, I chose to keep *Blessed Not Stressed* as the title represents a lifestyle we should all strive to live for.

As most of you know, I never hid the fact that I still write secular novels in a variety of genres. In today's world, my secular offerings outperform my faith offerings almost seven to one. What used to be a niche market name has gone on to diversify to incorporate many genres, including faith work. A lot of my readers who are familiar with my other works want to be introduced to gritty, faith-driven literature and I am proud to be able to provide this offering for them. For them, it allows them to follow characters they only see "in passing" and a way for me to introduce those who don't know Christ, to Him.

If you bought this book and you are getting another copy to support me and my literary efforts—I say "thank you" a thousand times. If you already have this book and don't wish to have a second copy, by all means return it— no harm, no foul. If you are new, welcome and I hope you enjoy my work.

I am proud to present *Blessed Not Stressed*, formerly published as *Love Him Like I Do*.

In Unity,

Isaiah David Paul

Fall 2001

A Prelude

As I stood before the pastor looking to give my life and my soul to The Master, I quickly turned around to glance at all of the people who were in attendance for my baptism. I could not believe all of these people came to Grace United Methodist Church to see. The small red brick church about a mile and a half from Winston-Salem State University, the city's HBCU.

I felt more nervous than an amateur performer at a talent show. With the sanctuary suited to accommodate about two hundred and fifty people, it seemed as though three times as many people found a way to be seated comfortably. When I came in an hour before Sunday school was to begin, the dining area, which accommodated another two hundred and fifty people was already packed with people sitting at round gold and blue clothed tables. Their eyes were glued to the rented 72" Samsung flat screen television, to broadcast the event that many in Winston-Salem, never thought would happen. I felt like everyone showed up to see and make a spectacle of what should've been one of the joyous occasions of my life.

Maybe if it weren't for whom I was, and what I used to do, my family and I could have enjoyed this occasion in the manner most pleasing to God. Personally, I didn't want the earthly celebration. But the fact of the matter was I couldn't change what I did, I could only desire to move forward with the Lord and let him lead me and guide me, as the choir sings, along the way. Besides I wasn't standing at the altar in front of all of these people to be seen, I was standing, with tears sneaking out of my eyes for Him.

This very moment, I was joining a physical church, devoted to being a productive member of The Body and to do as Jesus said, "go out into the world and make disciples." My heart was beating faster than the Luke Campbell songs I used to dance and perform to. I was scared that Jesus was going to come raise the roof and lift me out of the church. And even though I felt Jesus' presence and I felt protected, I could tell that the devil was busy, too. He probably was responsible for more than half of the people who had shown up that morning dressed to the nines and flashing cameras. I hadn't seen so many cameras flashing and lights shining since I was on the set of a video shoot. Some of the visitors probably wanted to see if I was really going to go through with this or if this was just an act or some sort of perverted scheme to advertise my former services in the church.

I didn't play with God like that when I wasn't saved, so why would I do that now?

But I digress—I had been attending Market Street A. M. E. Zion in Greensboro while I was at school but this was the first time I felt like I was an imposter trying to receive some of God's glory. Maybe folks had been there all along trying to see the circus too, but being within walking distance of A&T, Bennett and NC Tech, Market Street A. M. E. Zion was also two times larger in size than Grace and was packed with college students from around the city.

When I thought about all of the things I'd done, I allowed the deceiver to make be believe that I had stolen someone else's spot. That this salvation and celebration of my commitment to the Lord wasn't mine but perhaps belonged to one of the witnesses in the crowd. Yet, at the moment that thought crossed my mind, I rebuked it in the name of Jesus…just like the Pastor had told me to.

"Okay Jesus, you win," I felt my spirit saying to the Lord. I was claiming that victory as my mind flashed back to the days when I had been running from Him. For three years when He first pegged my heart after I'd boldly defiled a church with my actions and then published what I had done for the world to see while profiting from it hand over fist, He'd come after me. Not to condemn me, but to save me. That confused me at first because most people who'd done what I'd done surely would've been stoned. Of course, I thought He was lying to me just as everyone else had. And for a while, it appeared that He would allow me to continue running, going off and doing my own thing. In my running, I never thought about Him being omniscient, or the possibility that He would catch up to me. Like most young people, I wanted to enjoy what I thought was *my* life. I wanted to fit in and chase a few women just to see how many I could get at before I settled down. I wanted to try them all, no matter what color, size, social standing or level of comfort. I had something between my legs that I didn't know how to contain and I wasn't willing to learn how to tame. In many ways, I felt that it was worse than that little muscle they call the tongue. And not just that, I had a few "other" things I wanted to experience before I gave my life to Jesus. The way I saw it, I foolishly thought that once I got older, like past thirty five, I would have done everything that *I* wanted to do. I would have experienced everything that life had to offer and only after I had some ups and downs and some bruises, then I'd have what I needed to be knowledgeable and could begin serving Him. It was foolish of me, to think that I could run from or fight Him forever. I should have known that He already won and that this calling He was placing on me was to get my life together. Be a better man. Serve Him.

It seemed that when I was running the hardest, that's when I noticed the nightmares. The ones that always seemed to smell like burnt chitterlings mixed with a chemical fire but worse. The ones that had always ended with me dying a horrible death that I couldn't seem to stop from taking place. It seemed that the more horrendous way I died, the more vivid my path to Hell had become. Then there were these voices calling, screaming.

"Donte! Donte! Come join us."

I'd look at those ugly creatures and tried to run away but as I kept running from Jesus, it would appear that I kept running toward them instead.

"Lord, I'm sorry! I want to be saved! Please say it's not too late! I'll change!"

As I ran toward them, the merciful ones who'd only seemed to learn *after the fact* the true cost of their sins, I seemed to be mumbling…screaming the words after them. As they continued calling and screaming, my soul would begin to tremble. I tried to touch my body but it didn't feel the same. I knew I was me, but was not as I had been accustomed to. I was on fire and as I ran toward a lake that I hoped to jump in to save what remained of my flesh. My pain would take over and consume me as I, too, would continue in the screaming, the shouting.

There were days when I realized I was in a nightmare but now my eyes were locked and I couldn't find the keys. I, along with the millions who had a similar fate would scream and yell at the top of our lungs but He could not hear us. We knew that we were separated from Him forever, but we had hoped, dreamed that He didn't mean forever.

I most likely would have avoided all of this if I had just listened to some of my friends who had been trying to feed me the word of Jesus. The persistent ones who planted the Jesus seed and had prayed that despite my sinful occupation that their work would not be in vain and that their seeds would grow in my tarnished and infertile soil. A few had just trusted that if they planted the seeds, Jesus would take care of the rest. But some were more bold and radical than others. As they were planting and watering the soul I thought I had let go, my flesh had declared war on them. Paddles, torpedoes, nuclear missiles, machetes and daggers, I had thrown or swung them all at them. I gave it my best shot. I was so good I had built my own prison and locked myself in it, thinking I could make them go away. But that man Jesus, He would just walk in like He owned the place. And they, my friends, would stand right there next to Him.

"*Why don't you just give me a chance, Donte? I can give you more than you think you have now*," His spirit was telling me.

"I'm my own man," I would foolishly reply, "I've gotten all this on my own. What do I need you for?"

I would boldly take out my wallet and somehow, I was able to pull out pictures of all my worldly possessions. He would watch, nod His head and when I was finished reply.

"*For all that you think you have I can give you so much more. I AM the way, the truth and the life.*"

"What can you give me that I don't already have?"

The Son of Man replied…no, He whispered in my ear, "*Salvation.*"

I would think about it. Images of my family being poor, happy, keeping my life free from the love of money and being content with what I had all came to mind. That wasn't what I wanted. He knew this and then He would reply, "*It is easier for a camel to go through the eye of a needle than it is for a rich man to get to heaven.*"

I had been insulted. I worked hard for my riches and sacrificed quite a bit to get what I have. I even had to detach myself from my work. As I looked at Him, I realized He had quit talking and that my friends were praying for me. Then I heard voices, sounded like an argument was going on all around me. I kept looking around trying to identify the voices but I couldn't identify them. As I looked around at all the faces, I could hear the voices but couldn't see their lips move. The more I searched, the louder the voices got. I moved toward the crowd and there He was, following me. I looked over to the left and as the voices got louder, I followed in the direction. I looked over to my left and I could feel this energy, pulling me, trying to tear me apart. I looked over to my left and I was walking and running, falling and getting up. Working myself into a dizzy spell, all of a sudden one voice was clear…barely louder than a tweet.

"Be still and know that I am God."

When I stopped moving there was silence. I sat down Indian-style as I attempted to brace myself for this encounter. But I didn't see or feel Him. I expected this ultra-violent magnetic force—something like I would've seen in a movie, yet, everything was almost as it was before.

"Go to Ezekiel's room and tell him you are ready to talk.

"That's it?" Well, that sounded easy. I could do that. I had figured that he was still up studying for a test. But there was one small problem. I woke up to the evidence of my latest sin snoring lightly as I sat up and tried to squint my eyes open. "Well Lord, what do I do with the lady in my bed? I can't leave her in my room by herself."

"Take her home."

"Um, Lord," I was so embarrassed, "What is her name?"

If I didn't know any better, I could have sworn He was laughing at me. This wasn't the first time I had brought a woman to my bed and had been unable to remember her name after I had had my way with her. *"Ask her and she will tell you."*

And just like that my eyes were opened. I felt a strong powerful kick to my side and my nude chestnut-colored, six foot frame almost flew from my bed. I fought to hold on to the side of the bed, which was about a foot off the ground. I wasn't about to break a bone in my body landing on the mat that I had placed on the ceramic tile floor in my dorm room.

"Who are you?" she asked grabbing the sheets and pulling them up to cover her chest, as if she were in *her* bed and she didn't know how I had gotten there. I scooted over and raised my hand to put it over my eyes. My feet found the ground and I was able to sit up. I reached down to grab my pants and put them on but then I remembered that all of my clothes were near the door. I looked at my torso and then again at the floor and I shook my head in shame for not being able to find the condom that I thought we had worn hours before. I turned and placed my feet on the mat then walked to the dresser to get my boxer briefs that I snatched off the stereo. I was in such a rush to get into her that I must have flung it there when we hastily rushed in to do what we did.

"I'm Donte, who are you?"

"Eve."

"I gotta take you home," I finished putting on my clothes as Eve rushed to get her clothes on. She cursed me out and called me everything but a child of God for not remembering her name, despite the fact that it was tattooed over her bare shoulder. I wasn't trying to look at her because I didn't want to be tempted. And excuse me for trying to respect her sanctity while she was still topless in my room. I was trying to take baby steps to prove to the Lord that I was serious about what I was about to do. Normally, the situation would have turned out differently if a lady had managed to stay in the room at two o'clock in the morning, but I had a feeling that nights like that would not be occurring again anytime soon. I could tell that times were definitely changing.

We didn't bother to creep out of the dorm room despite the fact that we were in clear violation of co-ed visitation for her being on the male side of the dorm. Eve rolled her eyes when we got to my silver Lexus LS 430 and she slammed the door. A part of me wanted to curse her out, but I felt a calm working over me. I exhaled quietly to myself and let it go as I drove Eve to her dorm. As she got out, she slammed the door to my car again and instead of saying goodbye, she threw up her middle finger in my direction. I couldn't blame her for being mad at me.

As I drove to Ezekiel's room, I seen all these people giving me shout outs and praises and asking me when my next video was going to be out and who would be the next woman in it. I couldn't tell them that there would be no more videos. I got out of my car and walked to Ezekiel's room and banged on the door. You usually didn't do that at this time of night unless it was an emergency, which was the case then because my salvation was at stake. I turned the knob to find the brother on his knees deep in prayer at his bedside.

"Donte, what's up man? What's wrong?"

"I'm ready to talk about Jesus," I responded, almost out of breath.

Just like that I felt the weight lifting off my shoulders. I looked around and I could have sworn I saw angels rejoicing in heaven. Then I looked at Ezekiel, who was getting off his knees, and he hugged me.

"Praise God! Praise God! Hallelujah, my boy going to be saved! I've been waiting a long time for this day!"

Ezekiel took down a paperback book with some kids skating on it. He handed the book to me and told me to pull out the teal bookmark. I sat down at his desk and read the "Plan of Salvation" and I accepted Jesus as my Lord and Savior and asked him to come into my life. Ezekiel and I talked about Him all night. We talked about my past and what I was getting ready to give up and where I was getting ready to go in order to move forward.

It was one of our conversations as true friends that led me to my baptism as I looked into the crowd of what appeared to be a thousand member congregation. We had originally considered having a private ceremony but like an idiot, I decided against it. I wanted to be treated like any other new Christian. I hadn't taken into consideration that I was a "star." That was the *real* reason so many of the students and various other members of the community in the pews.

If it weren't a sin to bet, I'd gamble that majority of the women and men had seen me in videos—all in my nakedness doing things with other people's wives and daughters that I had no business doing. I was trying to justify it by saying that hopefully the married people would be "entertained" and "learned something new" to spice up their dull relationships. I may have looked like a rock star to them, but I felt like a baby scared to take his first steps. My knees felt weak and my flesh wanted to run out of the church and back to the things it was used to doing. It wanted to see the money it used to make just for a few hours of work. It loved the luxury of the life I was living in the Piedmont Triad that most people can only get in California. My flesh wanted everything that my conscious and the Holy Spirit made me sell and give up.

To my surprise my mother, father and younger brother had been standing behind me as well as a few sponsors. I didn't know if they had quite forgiven me for the life that I used to live or a small part of my flesh wanted to live but none of that mattered. I knew that if they were standing by my side, if they hadn't forgiven me yet, then their forgiveness was sure to come. Elicia Edmonds, my longtime friend, was standing with my family. Our twelve year friendship that began in the third grade when her parents moved to Winston-Salem from Benton Harbor, Michigan had truly gone through the test of time. If no one in this church was behind what I was about to do, I didn't have to question that she was. After all, she was the one that planted the seeds for me to be here. Ezekiel was at my side as well and I smiled knowing that my best friends were with me.

The pastor called for me to take the vows that would bind me to Jesus and His Holy Kingdom forever. The Donte Longstocking that most people in this sanctuary knew and probably still enjoyed was breathing his last breath. I was going to kill him. When I told the pastor "I do," that Donte and I could never be one and the same. In the few minutes that were to come, I would be reborn as Donte Eugene Speaks. My parents had come up with that name on their wedding night when they were planning the children that they were going to have. I looked at my parents again and I could see the happiness on my mother's face like the one she had when I graduated from Reynolds High School. I was crying too. I was fighting the tears that wanted to make my face the new Niagara Falls and cleanse my soul. My father and brother had put their hands on my shoulder.

For a young woman, Elicia smiled at me like she was an older woman taking pride in a young man she helped raise. To some degree, she did raise me considering all the work she did just to get me here. All the arguments we had gotten into about the Lord and getting saved and going to Hell seemed to be in the past. After all, she had the Lord on her side and I was too much of a man to hit a girl and too scared to try and fight Him. I knew I wasn't going to win so I ran as fast as could, thinking that if I ran fast enough and long enough, He would go away, but somehow, He always seemed to be right in front of me. I'd look back and He was beside me. I'd look down and I was ashamed to admit that I only saw one set of footsteps and I was sure they didn't belong to the size eleven and a half Air Force Ones I had on.

Before I knew it, the pastor had one hand on my back and another on my face. I don't remember getting into the pool, but my feet were wet and my brand new black Arrow slacks were sticking to my legs like peanut butter to bread. I guess I should have told him I was scared of the water. I was already crying and I felt my body start to tremble. I wanted to fight against the water because I couldn't swim. I felt like the pastor was going to slam dunk me like Michael Jordan over Magic Johnson in his first NBA title game.

"I got you," a small, meek voice whisper in my ear. Sounded like one of the boys in the hood, but I knew that not to be true. They said Jesus meets us where we are at, so I wasn't surprised that His spirit was confirming what I already knew.

I was raised out of the water to a thunderous applause. My family was hugging me and I was coughing, trying not to choke. When I took a breath I smelled a new air-one that reminded me of honey, coconuts and mango. Then I realized that was the lotion that Elicia had on.

"Welcome to the church Donte. I knew you could do it!" I opened my eyes and realized I was hugging Elicia. As I looked around the church the congregation looked new to me. It seemed larger, as if I was part of something that transcended the physical building I was in. Then a smile crept on my face and I was happy.

Fall 2002

Fall 2002

Total Praise

O ne of the hardest things about leaving the old world behind is that I find that my past always finds a way to stay connected to me. Since I've given up making adult videos and spoken up about my change of faith, I've been asked to visit churches and attend Christian functions all over the East Coast, denouncing my past and speaking out about the sin of fornication. I don't take a lot of those offers because I didn't quit doing adult videos to get into the ministry—I quit because that's what God led me to do and I wanted to satisfy Him. That and I suffered from having faith smaller than the size of a mustard seed.

I lived the lifestyle but I didn't believe that most people thought my salvation was real. Also there were pastors and churches who publicly denounced my dedication, saying that the congregation at Grace United was tricked into being part of another elaborate video that would be used to embarrass the church once again. I felt bad about that because not only was I not forgiven by some of the believers, but I saw the predicament I put the church in.

A few years back, I lied to the pastor and deacon board to gain access to the sanctuary. I brought my film crew and they recorded while another adult video star cursed the pews, the sanctuary and the pulpit with our bodies. I'm ashamed to admit that I pretended to be the pastor and I pretended that my body was the word. That video probably played a part in a few people not finding their salvation. Worst off, prominently displayed identifying marks clearly showed that the video was filmed in the church. Some of the members in the church tried to sue me but I won because I had a well-written contract tilted heavily in my favor and I bragged about how they cashed the check.

Some of the members of the congregation were going to hold me to that for the rest of my life.

I did agree to make a guest appearance on a local Christian rap group's upcoming album. Ironically, I had been invited to do an interlude promoting Christian rap as a viable means to spread the gospel and the importance of not leaving anyone out who wants to be saved. Cali, the older "super producer" who reminds me of Teddy Riley in the looks department, was pressed for time to get the track finished because they only have three weeks before the album has to be mastered, but the group feels my message is an important one, so they are spending their own money for the studio time and my session.

"You want to wrap it up and take a break for an hour or two?" Cali asked from his production booth.

"Naw, I'll be okay. Turn the light on and kill the incense cause it's not working for me. This ain't like making videos."

Everyone got a laugh out of that. Usually I went in, did my thing and even the flaws made the films better. With this, we can't have any flaws. I had been invited to be on a number of rap artists' albums and a few videos, but this was for the Lord. I wanted Him to be pleased with what I produced when it was all said and done.

"Aight, kid."

They turned on the light and let the cinnamon and raspberry-flavored incense leave the room. Then the miracle happened. My mind became clearer and I was able to finish my part of the track in ten minutes. I looked at my watch and realized it was 2:30 in the morning and that I have to help with freshman orientation in a few hours. I knew I wasn't going to get enough sleep.

***

I kept having this nightmare that I had gotten Eve pregnant and was a horrible father to our son, who would hunt me down and murder me in cold blood for my misdeeds. I didn't remember hearing about Eve being pregnant during the rest of that school year. Then again, I spent so much of my time worrying about what people thought of me and trying to avoid people who would tempt me with private sex shows or cash for the latest porn releases until I had become a hermit. I'd only go to class, the cafeteria to eat and the library to study.

Several folks accuse me of being on line and pledging one of those fraternities.

Of course people approached me and ask for videos. They wanted to know how they could get famous like I once was. Everyone thought it was cool to be me. But I bet none of them would want this lifestyle if they knew how many times I went to the clinic to get stuck by needles to make sure I produced negative HIV and STD results. I bet dudes wouldn't go through with getting swabs entering their tips, checking for pus and diseases. I bet none of the guys would spend the time in the gym that I had spent just to make sure my body was right. None of them would get on a plane, fly out to Los Angeles, Atlanta or Philly, shoot a scene and fly back that same day so they could study for an exam that still had to be taken the following day. Maybe my problem was I made it look too easy.

But back to Eve, I wouldn't even know if she still attended NC Tech or if she transferred to some other school or if something else happened. At any rate, each and every time I have this nightmare, I wake up, apologize to the Lord for my sins and then pray for her and the safety of her family.

I was trying to sleep on the spare bed in Ezekiel's room as his sister, Nia, was helping him set up his side of the room. Fortunately for me, his roommate called him and told him that he wasn't going to be in until the first day of school. We were juniors and I couldn't see how Ezekiel was still dealing with roommates. Probably because once I got famous my first semester at Gilbert, I was able to command my own room and have had it that way ever since. Ezekiel, on the other hand always saw an opportunity to minister the Word to any and everyone who was willing to listen.

"I guess you are blessed for getting here first," I heard Nia tell Ezekiel. "I'm surprised you got this big ol' picture of Huey P. Newton—I hope he likes the Black Panthers. Um…Huey does look sexy sitting there with that gun and spear though. I wouldn't mind."

"Nia stop!" Ezekiel failed to refrain from laughing at his sister's lusting after the Civil Rights icon. "My roommate will be alright. We share this room and we already discussed that the poster can hang over his bed so I can see it."

Nia climbed on top of the bed I was sleeping on. I could feel the mattress sinking just a little bit and I could hear her fumbling with the masking tape.

"Ezekiel, Donte is going to kick your butt if he catches me standing over his head like this," I could feel her moving around my head maneuvering around the bed, "I should wait until he gets up to put this poster up. I don't want him to be looking up my skirt. But for real, you need to get down from there."

As I felt her place her foot close to my head, I grabbed her leg and looked up, trying to avoid a peek at her skirt. I had forgotten how fine Ezekiel's younger sister was. It had been a few years since I saw her and it was then I remembered the off the wall comment I made about her bootylicious behind when I wasn't saved. I quickly sat up.

"Oh my gosh," Nia yelled as she stumbled on the bed. She landed dead smack on her butt and we were face to face. I didn't realize how strong my grip was on her leg. "See Ezekiel, look at what you made me do, I done woke him up," Nia was embarrassed.

"I didn't tell you to get on the bed and put the poster up there. I told you to wait but you wanted to get up there."

I let go of his sister's leg.

"No that's okay. I wasn't asleep, I was resting," I assured her.

"Up all night, huh?" Nia inquired.

"Yeah, I was working with this Christian rap group on a track for their upcoming CD."

"Ooh…Christian rap group?! Which one?"

"Nia, get out of the man's business," Ezekiel scolded her.

"Naw, I don't mind," I answered. "The group I'm working with is trying to keep the production of their latest CD a secret because they don't want everyone to know they are back home working on their CD."

"Oh, I know who it is now," Nia smiled. After I thought about it, I realized that I did just tell their secret. I hope they forgave me. "Don't worry Donte, I'm not going to go around town telling the business. I'm just glad you aren't making those videos no more."

"I'm not the average boy on the video," I started singing a line from the popular India.Aire song. "Naw, it's been almost a year since I've made a video."

"I'm glad. I got tired of having to come up with tales and having to explain how folks could hear Ezekiel giving directions in some of the videos."

If looks could kill, Nia would be dead. Not too many people were supposed to know that Ezekiel was in some of the earlier videos…sorta. Nia got off the bed and got ready to leave.

"Well Donte, I got to take my sister home."

"Aight man, I'll still be here."

"Bye Mr. Porn Star," Nia waved at me flirtatiously.

"Bye Nia."

Ezekiel walked Nia to the door. "Ezekiel you should have told me you were going to room with someone famous. You should have made Donte move in with you."

"So you can flirt with him and put both of y'all in sin's way? No, thank you. I value my friendship with my boy and I know he won't do that to me."

Nia turned around and seen that I was still standing at the door watching them too. "Come to Bennett with me. Y'all can help me set up my room."

"I don't think that's a good idea. Some of those girls know who I am and I'm kinda not allowed back there." My mind quickly raced to a scene in one of my movies where we were getting down in a very visible spot on campus. The president had to issue an apology to the alumni and I had to settle with them out of court to keep them from suing me. They had taken a sizable portion of my fortune and that's one of the few videos I'd ever done that I had lost the rights to.

"Don't be ridiculous, I need all the help I can get setting up my room and besides, Zeke owes me."

Ezekiel rolled his eyes and shook his head. I knew I'm one of the "crushes" that she has, but she knows I wouldn't go for her. One, cause Ezekiel is my best friend. Two, I thought she had a man at A&T—it seems like all the girls there do, or at least that's what they told us. And three, I needed to focus on my relationship with God and keeping Mini Me in my pants.

"I'm going to head out. We can meet back up for dinner before we have Bible study."

"Cool."

We all left Ezekiel's room. I headed toward the front office to volunteer to help the freshmen move into the neighboring dorm. After I had signed up and had been given a Dorm Helper T-Shirt, I walked outside my dorm to see that the parking lot was packed as proud parents of college freshmen were moving their young adult's stuff into their new homes.

"Got your room all set for college?" I heard an older man ask the girl ahead of me.

"Yep, it's almost done, just a few more things."

"It's good to see such a fine young lady going off to college. I mean it took forever for me to convince your older brother to go to college."

"Now, how was you going to go tell somebody to go to college when you didn't go yourself?" the lady with them asked. I tried to hold back a smile.

"Well, let's see, I moved out of the shack and once I got one into college, the rest of those hard-headed children knew they had to follow."

It's interesting to listen to grown folks talk, well, at least some of them. You got around the right ones and they'll relive history, the moments and forget the audience around them.

As I escaped the older man's tale, I noticed the moving truck coming up the street. Coming out of the driver's seat was a red-haired black girl. Now from here, it doesn't look like it is dyed with black streaks in it but natural red hair. I had to get up close to see for myself. She was helping a young lady in a Dorm Helper T-Shirt move some boxes into her dorm. When I got across the street, I realized that the red-haired woman was Daisy Roxboro. I'm surprised I remember her name because I hadn't seen her in a long time and I didn't remember her being so bold. The Daisy I remembered was one of those quiet reserved girls who barely got into trouble. When she looked across the street, she glared at me with piercing onyx eyes and at that moment, something in my spirit jumped. I tried to discern whether or not she or I were in trouble or if my mind was playing tricks on me. Either way, something in my spirit wasn't right. The next time I caught a glance at her, everything was calm and her face seemed friendlier then it had before. Maybe I was wrong about what I had seen before.

***

"You are coming to the dinner time Bible study in the cafeteria tomorrow aren't you?" Ezekiel asked once we were back in my room putting my things away. I had just come from Winston-Salem, bringing some of the clothes I had washed and dried that were in suitcases in my room. When I opened the suitcases, I could still smell the fresh scent the fabric softener left behind.

"Yeah man, hopefully when I come around this time, we'll actually be able to study the Word as opposed to fielding questions about why I'm not making videos." I said as I started putting some of my polo and button up shirts on hangers.

"Man, I wouldn't even worry about that. Besides, Rahliem Victor from the Street Disciples Ministry is coming so maybe he'll be able to help us with any crowds."

"That name sounds familiar," I reflected but still couldn't draw a face to the name.

"I'm excited. This brother has only been out of prison for only a year and some change and he is making radical changes for how young people participate in church ministries," Ezekiel replied as he stacked some of the Bibles, devotion and faith fiction literature that I had brought with me on the book case. "I really think you two would be a good match and that he may be able to share some things with you on how to move forward with your walk in Christ."

"Prison?" I didn't mean to sound so judgmental but I was definitely interested in hearing about how and why this brother got in prison.

"He used to have anger management problems and when he was seventeen, he almost killed a young man who tried to bully his younger brother because of his sexuality."

"Oh."

"But Rahliem's been on the up and up since he's been in prison and now that he's out, he's really doing big things. Though he is a member of Grace United, he's working with some of the leaders of the other churches to help them strengthen their youth ministries and prepare more young people for theology school."

"I didn't know he was a member of Grace." That bothered me that this man who was doing great things was a member of my home church and I hadn't met him yet.

"That's because you spend a lot of your time at Market Street—even in the summer time."

"Yeah, but I did that so I could work more with some of the student ministers and faith leaders here. We needed representation here over the summer with all the colleges doing summer orientations and some of the youth based festivities."

"True, and that was good. Plus, I know you were in summer school, too."

"Right, that year I spent building my business did put me behind academically from where I needed to be. Plus, I did decide to take on another major because anymore, a brother needs more than one degree to make it in this world."

"You're right about that."

"At any rate, I'm looking forward to meeting Rahliem and seeing what the brother has to offer."

Ezekiel hung up the rest of my clothes while I finished setting up my computer system. I saw the clock and realized that he had to go lead a Bible study in a dorm on A&T's campus. He and I gave each other a pound and he walked out of the door. I would've gone with him, but I need to get my room situated. With school starting soon, I don't have much time to get things together. I know if he needs me, he'll call and I am cool with that. After making sure the computer, my laser printer and my scanner were hooked up correctly, I took the paperback Bible off the bookshelf and began reading Exodus. I loved reading the Old Testament stories and imagining how people lived back then before all of this technology. After an hour of getting caught up with Moses and everything he'd done to lead our people out of Egypt, I placed a neon green flyer that served as a $5 off coupon for a large pizza at one of the local restaurants in the Bible to keep my place. I walked to the head of my bed, got on my knees, and thanked the Lord for allowing me to live to see another day. Then I stripped off my clothes, got in my extra long twin sized bed and went to sleep.

I Know It Was the Blood

I met with Ezekiel and Elicia for breakfast at the Reginald F. Lewis Cafeteria. The two-floor auditorium sized building is large enough to easily accommodate five hundred students at once. The glass panels can almost be mistaken for mirrors, as some of the students stopped to look at their reflections and fixing themselves up before going in. They were oblivious to the fact that those sitting at the tables and booths could see them primping and priming.

The cafeteria only complimented the "old school meets new school" vibe of the buildings on a campus that sat on one hundred and seventy five acres. Some of the dorms we live in are all brick buildings built in the 1950's with renovations to the interior done in the seventies and eighties. They vary between two and three stories high and are scattered on the north and south ends of campus. The school buildings were slowly becoming modernized. The science building has a gigantic telescope at the top that could be seen from half a mile away as if it were part of downtown Greensboro's skyline. Our football stadium easily accommodates 35,000 fans and is large enough to rival some stadiums used by NFL teams. The School of Business and Economics building is connected to the School of Law by a bridge, which is convenient when it is cold outside for us to enter one building and walk through to the other. The Student Union is a glass and steel building that sit on a hill with steps leading to its entrance similar to the steps of the Lincoln Memorial. The other schools and dorms compliment the magnificent view of this higher institution of learning.

The smell of chicken and waffles that Roscoe's is known for permeated the air and made me hungrier. I haven't had chicken and waffles since I was in L. A. for a "special video shoot." I can't wait to wrap the homemade blueberry waffles around the fried chicken strips and dunk them in the maple syrup. It is my guilty pleasure and I know I'm going to pay for it with a few laps around campus, a couple of dates with a bench press and the exercise bike. The inside the cafeteria looks the size of a football field and then some. Lines to get the plates aren't that long…it's just a lot of people in the cafeteria.

For a university that has almost ten thousand students, it should be like this. Last year, we ate in mobile trailers while they re-modeled the cafeteria and I attended the grand opening ceremony where they named it after the man who founded the TLC Group, which specialized in investing in and selling highly profitable ventures. His biggest would become TLC Beatrice International Holdings, Inc, a manufacturer of processed meats, dairy products and beverages. Like most buildings at an HBCU, NC Tech tried to name all of their buildings either after prominent administrators for the schools or a trailblazer that usually was not recognized until Black History Month—if they received any notoriety then.

On our way to the table, I noticed some of the fellas gawking at Elicia's statuesque five foot six frame with smooth butterscotch colored skin. Her hair was shoulder length and twisted like licorice. The eyes were somewhat Orient in nature, partially because her father is half Cherokee, but they remind me of almonds. Her nose and mouth both fit lovely on her face and they give her the look of an ancient Egyptian goddess. Her body was slim and the lustful side of me would admit curvaceous in all the right places. If I weren't saved, I'd lick my lips, make my move instead of staring at her.

When I got to the table where everyone was meeting, I was surprised to see a young man sitting in the middle of the group with an A-line T-shirt with his muscles and prison tattoos exposed. His heavy weight boxing frame brought to mind Evander Holyfield in his prime. His braids and sharp goatee added to the stereotypical prison look it appeared that many youth and young adults in our communities had fallen in love with. His sharp, wood carved features matched his walnut colored skin.

The closer I got, I could see that his pants were baggy, but not hanging off his behind and he was wearing black Nike slide shoes with white socks. He doesn't look like the kind of guy who'd hang with a church group, but out on the benches or on some of the stoops trying to holla at the women walking around on campus. I saw the way some of the women who were sitting in the vicinity where his table was looked at him the way they looked at me—with lust.

"Donte," Ezekiel stood and walked to me. "This is Rahliem, the brother I was telling you about who started the Street Disciples Ministry out of Grace United Methodist Church."

Rahliem stood to shake my hand and I was surprised that the man was the same height as I. In spite of his harden look, Rahliem's smile was infectious and I could tell the man was blessed as I felt the spirit of God around him.

"I'm glad I finally get to meet the star," Rahliem greeted as he sat back down. I put my tray across from his and realized that I had forgotten to get a juice drink. I'd deal with that later. "I saw a video of the baptism man, I hate I missed it."

Were people selling videos of my baptism? I was skeptical. This was the first time I had ever heard of there being a video because I had never seen it.

"Yeah, it was definitely a sight to see."

"Well, when you get a chance, I'd like to talk with you more about Street Disciples soon and give you a chance to see us out in the community doing work. I think you'd be a great addition and I think some of the young men whom I work with would look up to you."

I nodded my head. I'm careful about promising to participate in someone's ministry because I feel like I'd be lying to God and that was the last thing I wanted to do. Other students found the table where the Bible Study was soon to be held. For the next few minutes, everyone at the table ate and just socialized as they confirmed classes and talked about upcoming events on campus. Ezekiel was writing some stuff down and taking notes. Elicia arrived and she sat next to me.

"I'm on the verge of making a big decision," she confided in me, "I've thought about this decision for a long time but I'm not sure if I'm completely ready for the mission at hand. It's a tedious job and an enduring campaign that I don't want to lose my soul to in the process."

In all my years of knowing Elicia, I had never known her to be scared or even slightly touched by anything, except for the possibility that I would break her heart, again. "Elicia, I'm sure that whatever undertaking you are considering will be one that will make you stronger, no matter the outcome." I tried to make her smile. "You are the epitome of a Proverbs 31 woman. Most women wish they had what you possess."

"Thank you. I wish I could tell you more about it but it's a surprise. I haven't even told Mary yet." Mary Braxton was Elicia's best friend and confidant. She stretched the limit of creativity with her Miriam and Mary clothing line. "I'll make an announcement about it next Sunday. It may not even surprise you but I want to make sure it's the right decision and that I take it to the Lord in prayer before I start telling everyone that's what I want to do."

As I looked over at Ezekiel, I noticed that he had written a poem. Ezekiel's handwriting was so small it looked as it if were one continuous line. I didn't try to read it, for they say it is not a good look to read a poem before it's ready. My attention being brought back to Elicia, I watched as she picked up a piece of chicken and some waffles and gracefully guide the fork to her mouth. I pinched her cheek for old times' sake in hopes of making her laugh.

"Gosh, boy, you are going to stop doing that."

Elicia noticed her two line sisters, Gabrielle and Aaliyah making their way toward the table to sit next to us. She got up and embraced each of them and sat down to continue eating her meal. They occupied two empty chairs next to her. Aaliyah was a tall, slender looking girl with dark chocolate skin and long hair whose features epitomized what the Europeans thought of as beautiful. Gabrielle, on the other hand, was representing for the big girls with her round features that evenly supported her thick frame.

"Let me find out that you two were sharing a moment," Aaliyah teased, "do I need to leave you alone?"

"No Aaliyah, you know it's not even like that. Donte is my friend, remember?"

Of course Aaliyah would remember, she reminds me every chance she gets at how tight *we* used to be. Our affair lasted briefly and the main source of her fascination with me was that I was in all the videos. She didn't even want anyone to know that we were being intimate—not dating because we weren't fully committed. I knew she had a man and I was still doing videos. When Aaliyah got saved, she cut me off and when she and Elicia later became friends, I promised myself I'd never tell Elicia what happened between Aaliyah and I.

"I am so ready for this year to get started. Next week can't get here soon enough," Gabrielle commented.

"Yeah, it's about that time in our lives when summer is going to be over and the school year is about to begin, thank you Jesus," Aaliyah added.

"Yep, we are juniors this year and whatever decisions we make about education and other personal endeavors will have the potential to shape the rest of our lives," Gabrielle continued. "I'm so glad that I don't have to be in that cafeteria today. I want to enjoy my last day of freedom before I have to get to work."

"Amen to that."

During Bible Study, we focused on Matthew 7:1-5 which talks about judgment. I felt some form of conviction because my first thought of Rahliem was "what was he doing here?" With his dress, the tats and the hairstyle I would have either pegged him as a new freshman who hadn't been groomed yet or I would've assumed him to have been a street thug that a lot of these girls seem to be attracted to nowadays. I would have missed an opportunity to get to know or possibly work with a man of God. Yet, those verses also resonated with me because a lot of people still judge me by the videos I used to make and the parties I used to participate in and have yet to meet the Holy Spirit that resides inside of me.

After our short Bible study, we finished eating our food and then we left the cafeteria. It truly was our last day of freedom and then classes would start tomorrow. I have my classes on Tuesdays and Thursdays all day. I didn't have anything to do so I walked the ladies back to their dorms and then Ezekiel and I hung out in his room and prayed that as we began another year at NC Tech, that it would be a successful and prosperous year.

I Want Jesus To Walk With Me

I was waiting in my cinnamon colored 1985 Lincoln Continental for Elicia to come down the stairs of the church. I felt a little guilty about missing the third service since I got saved and baptized last year. I was hoping Jesus didn't mind. I probably should've gone but truthfully, I didn't want to deal with my car. When I gave up most of my worldly possessions I had gotten from selling the adult videos I was in, I downgraded from a Lexus to a Continental. For me, part of the reason I chose the car was because it wasn't fancy. I thought that by getting an older car, I'd be showing humility. I've had it for about a year now and the light on the speedometer doesn't work, so I not only not know how many miles I'm going per hour, I couldn't tell you how much gas I have in the car. The right passenger window doesn't roll down anymore, which has become a gift and a curse. The twenty year old interior was in serious need of an upgrade. I was able to find nice, plush, tan colored seat covers, which did a great job of hiding the cuts and discoloration of the original seats. Ezekiel and Nia joked that my "new" car looked the way a well-used Bible should look when it's been used properly. After waiting on her for fifteen minutes, Elicia was talking to one of the other church members and carrying on. I took it to mean she enjoyed the service.

"Donte, could you take Mary to the dorms?" Elicia commanded moreso then asked as she took her spot in the front seat. Mary's crimson hat almost fell off while she was getting in the car and she almost fell in the seat trying to hold her hat. Mary was an aspiring fashion designer who looked like she could pass for one of the ladies in EnVogue. She made her own clothes, including the black and white zebra-striped number she had on now. I'm not going to lie she was talented, but she also had a nasty attitude. She came off as one of those people that felt like she could have been in the book *Our Kind of People*. True to herself she acted as if she came from the type of black folks who had old money and could look down at you because you were darker than a paper bag.

"You should have opened the door, Donte," Mary criticized me. I saw her eyes piercing at me in my rearview window.

"It's alright," Elicia defended me, "I'm the one catching the ride."

"But he's supposed to be the *man* and not just on camera. That's what's wrong with our black men now— they don't know how to treat a lady."

See, if I had gotten out of the car and opened the door for her, she probably would've been on this independent woman craze that Beyonce and them children got these other girls on. Lately I've noticed that when a man shows chivalry and "acts like a man" it's not appreciated. I could have driven off and left her on the steps of the church and she could have walked to school for all I cared. It's sad that even after a year and some change since getting saved and giving up the old life, people are still going to remind me about the videos. I guess they'll live on, even though I have been a changed man. I pulled away from the church and headed to the school. In retrospect, the drive was really short and a walk wouldn't have hurt anybody. I thought about that as we drove past Bennett College, which enrolled only female students. Other students who had attended the church were talking and socializing and heading toward the cafeteria for brunch. This was definitely a day that I wished the passenger window rolled down.

"Eww, what is this?" Mary whined, working what I was sure was my last nerve. She held her hand on the front and some brownish black oil smudge like grease was on the tips of her fingers. "I hope this isn't on my hat or my clothes Donte because if it is, you're paying for it."

I offered her some napkins and a hand sanitizer, praying that would be the remedy for the new drama she seemed to find herself in. I was happy that her dorm was near the entry of the school. When she got out, Elicia got out with her and they spent a minute by the car inspecting her outfit and helping her get cleaned up. I just shook my head because Mary didn't even bother to say thank you. Then again, what else should I have expected from these New Age prima donnas trying to take over the campus?

"You are coming to my meeting tonight aren't you?" Elicia asked as she was getting her bible and the small bag she was carrying together and opening the door.

"You know I will be there," I replied. Truthfully, I had forgotten that Elicia had said something about the meeting a week ago. Classes had begun and we were already knee deep into our studies. I had gone to meetings with Ezekiel about the new ministry he wanted to start on campus and also was focused on keeping all the freshmen who discovered that I was a "celebrity" from trying to follow me to and from classes. At the start of every school year since I was at Gilbert, freshmen students made it a scavenger hunt to figure out my class schedule and to hound me for autographs. When I was living for the world, I didn't mind as I had party fliers for the ladies with my near naked body on it that I signed with a permanent marker and I limited pictures-takings to five minutes as long as we weren't in the hallways. Once word had spread that I got saved and that I had stopped making movies, most of the fans seemed to disappear. Of course, a few people tried to "challenge me" on my knowledge of Jesus and the Bible to see what Bible verses I knew and whether or not I was faking the funk. I think by the end of that fall semester, everyone knew I was serious and respected my judgment to follow Jesus. At the start of the spring semester, as well as in summer school, the only people who were looking for me were the new students or those who had ditched a class at one of the nearby universities to come find me.

"I want you to be there. And don't be late either." Elicia closed the door before I could respond. I don't know why she thought I would miss her meeting, but I guess it was really important that I be there.

***

We met in one of the conference rooms in the library. I had brought one of my Bibles because knowing Elicia, she would be referencing the book at some point during our meeting. Aaliyah and Gabrielle were sitting in the front row. Aaliyah was the first to roll her eyes at me. Gabrielle still had on her hairnet from cooking the brunch we ate in the café. I forgot what she majored in, the only time I really saw her was when she was in the café or when she was doing a function with their sorority. Ezekiel walked in with some more of Elicia's sorority sisters. Some of his line brothers rolled in and I shook each of their hands. A few other students we knew were coming in and soon, the conference room was filled.

Elicia walked in moments later sporting a pinstriped business suit with a matching hat and some shades. As she made her way to the front, people rose and clapped for her. I'm not going to lie, she looked stunning. The big bouncy curls were a lot different than the straight hair she wore to church earlier today. She walked to the podium that had been placed at the front of the conference room earlier and she placed her hat on the table beside Aaliyah.

"Brothers and sisters and friends, good evening."

"Good evening."

"This evening, September 15, 2002, I look forward to building a team that will help me succeed in a great undertaking. Before I start, can we open our Bibles to Psalms 134? Aaliyah, could you lead us in our reading?"

As everyone ruffled through their Bibles to the verse, a young lady came to me and inquired about borrowing mine. I didn't have an extra one, so I put mine between us so that we could share. We looked on as Aaliyah read, *"Come, bless the LORD, all you servants of the LORD, who stand by night in the house of the LORD! Lift up your hands to the holy place, and bless the LORD. May the LORD, maker of heaven and earth, bless you from Zion."*

We sat down after Aaliyah read the Word. Elicia took her place at the podium.

"For two and a half years, I have watched you, prayed with you, pledged with you, and worked with you as we worked to spread the Word of Jesus Christ and to make NC Tech students, faculty and staff more accountable and an active part of the Greensboro community. We have seen students come to this institution and have their lives change forever. We have seen students leave this institution and look back and think about where they've come from and we've reached a hand forward, with the thought of always looking after the previous generation. I feel that as we have become student leaders and upperclassmen of our university, it is time that we take our places so that we can continue the work that previous generations have laid before us. This evening, I request your support in being part of my team as I pursue the title of Miss North Carolina Technical University."

In a room full of claps, one could hear Ezekiel exclaim, "You getting started early ain't you?"

After the clapping died down, Elicia replied. "No, now is the time for us to get started. I was in this very room when our current Miss NC Tech, Arnisha Patterson announced her intentions to run for the title."

"That is what's up," Aaliyah announced.

"Do you know of anyone else running for the title?" Gabrielle asked.

"Well, it's not really a secret that Donlynne Winston intends to run for the title this year."

"The SGA secretary," the girl who was reading the Bible with me asked. Donlynne Winston was a sophisticated young lady almost in the same class as Mary. She was a tall, caramel colored beauty that reminded me of a younger looking Condoleezza Rice. Only difference between Donlynne and Mary is that in most cases, Donlynne could be down to earth. She's the type of woman that knows what she wants and knows how to get it and as long as it's not illegal, she'll get her way.

"Yes, Keisha, she is currently our SGA Secretary. And she will be a formidable opponent for all those who intend to run this year. She is already at work building her team and trying to gain the support of the Student Senate."

"Isn't that illegal?" Gabrielle asked. The thought had crossed my mind to ask the same thing, but I had held my tongue.

"Sure is, you know what? I'm glad you are running because I can't stand her." Aaliyah probably would have gone on if Elicia hadn't put her finger to her mouth. Donlynne and Aaliyah had a public spat over Malachai Watson, our current SGA President. Apparently, Mr. President was seeing both of the ladies last fall and that almost caused two of the sororities on the yard to have a public fight.

"Getting to Gabrielle's question, yes, what she is doing is illegal. Some would say that this meeting is illegal since this semester's grades are considered when calculating the 3.0 GPA all candidates must have to enter the race. Also, no candidate can turn in paperwork or publicly announce they intend to run until February."

"What's your GPA?" One of Ezekiel's brothers asked.

"I have a 3.25, but I feel confident that I will be eligible to run."

"Who else is running?" Aaliyah asked.

"I heard that Mary Braxton intends to run," Ezekiel mentioned.

Mary? I thought. We had just given that rude, selfish chick a ride back to her dorm this morning and now, this chick was gonna run against my friend.

"Yes, Mary does intend to run for the title as well. As some of you know, her sister was Miss NC Tech back in 1997. She is also our current Miss Junior."

"Doesn't Donlynne have a family legacy of being Miss NC Tech?" Gabrielle asked.

"She is looking to be a fourth generation Miss NC Tech," Elicia answered.

"Well between you and that girl, that ain't gonna happen," Aaliyah announced. Elicia looked at her again and Aaliyah collected herself.

"What I wanted to do is put together a committee that will explore the opportunities and help me with my plans to put together a campaign. I am trying to come correct, no half stepping."

"Amen to that," Ezekiel cheered, drawing laughter from the room.

"So who is going to be your campaign manager?" Gabrielle asked.

"I'm glad you asked. I have chosen Donte Eugene Speaks to be my campaign manager."

All heads turned and I could feel all eyes on me. Here I was being made the center of attention again. To think I used to like it but now. If I had a cup of drink it would have fallen to the ground. I was supportive of Elicia running for Miss NC Tech but the idea of being her campaign manager was another story. If I had been another person these past three years, I wouldn't have a problem considering it. And I didn't feel like having my past life dragged through the rumor mill again. Not to mention that I would have felt terrible if I knew that Elicia lost the campaign because of me.

"Un-uh," Aaliyah shook her head, being the first one to object. "Nothing against you Donte, but I don't think it would be in your best interest to select Donte *Longstocking* to be your campaign manager," I looked around the room and I could feel everyone staring at me. Thanks to Aaliyah and her big mouth, I was starting to feel nervous and uncomfortable.

"Give him a chance, Aaliyah. Donte got good business sense," Ezekiel defended.

"That may be well and good but you know as well as I know that people are going to associate his videos with her campaign. Are you sure you want that associated with your image?"

"You enjoyed the movies didn't you?" Ezekiel asked. A part of me couldn't believe that Ezekiel put Aaliyah on the spot like that—and being my best friend, I knew he had an ulterior motive for bringing that up. I gave him the side-eye. As I looked around I could see others in the room chuckle or try to pretend that they weren't embarrassed. If I were Caucasian, I wouldn't be able to hide my embarrassment.

"That's not the point," Aaliyah mumbled.

"Well, you can't take the mote out of his eye until you take the beam out of yours sweetie," Elicia smiled as she paraphrased a verse in Matthew and hugged Aaliyah. Aaliyah playfully pushed her away. "I'm sure we just read or talked about that a week ago. Anyway, this campaign is not about Donte *Speaks*." I liked how she emphasized my last name.

"This is about me. And how would I look telling everyone I'm a Christian and I am standing here passing judgment? I don't sit at the right hand of the Father, Jesus does. I would be a hypocrite if that were my sole reason not to use Donte's excellent negotiation and management skills for my campaign. The way I see it, if Donte used his skills to get good deals on advertisement and merchandising and I let him come up with a good fundraising plan, no one in this room will have to help me pay for the campaign."

Everyone's tune changed when she put it that way.

"When is our next meeting," Gabrielle asked.

"Everyone is to put their email addresses by their names and I will email you further instructions."

I watched the sheet of paper float around the room. Mary walked into the conference room and everyone almost stopped what they were doing. Why, I couldn't figure out but as Elicia went to meet her at the door, Aaliyah came up to me.

"You sure you know what you are doing? This campaign is a big responsibility, and I don't want you to mess it up for my girl."

"Elicia and I will work everything out. Have faith, princess."

She put her hand in my face and left the room. I couldn't believe I spent moments of intimacy with her and at that point in time, I started to truly understand why God required us to save sex until marriage. Gabrielle walked up to me, smiled and left. Ezekiel pulled me to the side to talk to me about a few of his boys and to see if I was coming to Bible study this evening. I passed because I knew I would be spending my time with Elicia getting ready for her campaign. Besides, we had a history paper that was due Tuesday, so we would work on that as well. When Elicia came back into the room, I pulled her to the side.

"Elicia, are you sure about this?"

"O ye of little faith Donte? If I didn't know that you were the best man for the job, I would have picked someone else. Those other people may have seen your videos. Others may have lusted after and had dreams about you. But it is *I* who knows you. You are my friend."

She kissed me on the cheek and left the room. I could see it now, me dressed down to the nines, accompanying Elicia everywhere she went on campus as she tried to engage the ten thousand students into caring about her cause and voting. I could see her name as well as mine in the paper as they focused on her issues and her being the perfect woman of faith to represent our institution on a local and national level. For a minute, I could see the naysayers holding up pictures of my body connected to other women or replaying my videos as a prank, but I also felt that forgiveness from Jesus that made the pictures and the videos disappear. From that moment on, I smiled.

Somebody Prayed for Me

I agreed to pick Mary, Elicia and Gabrielle up so we could meet and plan our Sickle Cell Anemia Fundraiser. Every year the SGA at NC Tech picked a charity or a cause and raised student awareness by education, seminars and some trivia and prizes. This year, we decided to do a fundraiser for the Sickle Cell Anemia Association that was down the street from the school. Sickle Cell Anemia is a blood disorder that affects predominantly African-Americans. There wasn't a cure for sickle cell but we hoped to address the issue of being tested to find out if you are a carrier for the trait.

I walked across the new housing complex that had been built off of Market Street in hopes of reaching Elicia's suite. She and Aaliyah agreed to be suite mates this year and they also shared a suite with a girl who went to A&T.

As I was walking to their door, I noticed a woman dancing and singing in her room. The windows were up and the lights were on. You could see this woman dancing in her undergarments. As I got closer, the song stopped and then another one came on. Aretha Franklin's "Don't Play That Song For Me" came on and she was just a dancing and singing.

Behind me, a small crowd was starting to form because this woman had a very powerful voice. She was deep into the song when I noticed her face. I felt bad for looking up at her in the window, as it seemed almost perverted. But my intent was not to lust after her sexually. This woman, whoever she was, had a really nice voice that commanded attention and she definitely had mine.

She put the song on repeat and she went into the song and dance movement. I remember seeing a video of the dance she was doing online somewhere and I have to admit, she did a very good job, hitting the old seventies number beat for beat. That's when R&B was somewhat innocent and you could listen to it after church. At least that was what my parents used to tell me. The crowd that had gotten larger continued to watch her sing and dance. Some were off to the side singing and dancing with her. There were a group of girls moving in step hitting the background vocals. I didn't even notice that I had tapped my feet or clapped my hands until I looked down. I was embarrassed at first and then I noticed that I wasn't alone. I looked around and seen the girls turn and twirl and continue to sing. They were a mess.

Then there was a loud knock on her door and she turned the music down. A collective awe came from the crowd. An older woman who looked like she could've passed for the young lady's mother stuck her head full of light green and orange rollers out of the window.

"The show's over! Go home!" She slammed the window shut.

The crowd was disappointed and kept singing the song as they moved away from the building. I thought the whole thing was a trip.

"Darling, I love you," Aaliyah was singing as she came up to me, taunting the girl in the window. "You couldn't come straight to the room could you?"

"I thought you were supposed to be at work?" I responded to avoid answering her question. I refused to admit that I had a legitimate excuse for being distracted.

"I am at work, making sure Elicia and Gabrielle get on their projects."

"Girl please," Gabrielle interrupted, "you are the one known to procrastinate."

"This is true," Elicia agreed.

"Forget both of y'all, in a few minutes, we was about to see the rebirth of Donte Longstocking."

I quickly looked down realizing that Aaliyah and the girls were laughing at me as she pulled another joke on me. That wasn't funny at all, but I couldn't stop grinning just the same.

"I feel for that girl," Aaliyah continued, "dancing in her undergarments like that and then to get caught by Ms. Simmons, in her rollers. Lord, have mercy, I know she was embarrassed."

"I bet she was."

We walked to the library, which happened to be a few blocks away. We were going to meet Ezekiel, Arnez and Keisha there. We were going to get the preliminary work done so that when the project was presented at the next executive board meeting, we could get it approved with a majority vote. The executive board for NC Tech's student government association consisted of the president, vice-president of internal affairs (also known as the president of the senate), vice-president of external affairs, the secretary, the treasurer, Miss NC Tech, the parliamentarian and the chief of staff. Of the two positions, only the parliamentarian and chief of staff were appointed by the president, everyone else was elected by the students of the university. Most of the students on the executive board got along with each other most of the time. This was definitely a benefit when it came down to planning events and getting different ideas together. It was obvious that they worked together as a unit and fought together to get the things we felt was best for our students. There was also another event that we wanted to work with A&T students on, but we needed to get our event together first.

"What's her name?" I asked.

"What's whose name?"

"The girl dancing in the window."

"Oh that's Faith. She is mad cool. She's about to graduate this year, too."

"Really? That's what's up."

I thought about Faith. The full figured sister seemed like she could be my type. I wondered what her major was and what plans she had once she got out of class. The thought crossed my mind to check to see if she was saved because that was the only way we were going to have a real future together.

***

"So did you think about joining Street Disciples?" Ezekiel asked after we wrapped up our research on the Sickle Cell Anemia project. We were leaving the library and I felt guilty because I hadn't thought about Rahliem or Street Disciples since we last spoke to him in the café. I shook my head no. "Man, that's okay. He's supposed to be coming up here tomorrow. You'll be able to give him an answer then."

"Yeah but this shouldn't have slipped my mind." I was frustrated. "I mean, I was quick to help Elicia with her campaign to become Miss NC Tech, quick to consider getting Faith's number, quick to do this project but when it was time for me to think about the Lord, I put it to the side."

"Donte, you can't beat yourself up every time you sin." Ezekiel laughed at me and I was offended. I felt some kind of way about not always jumping to serve the Lord when the opportunity struck. "If you start doing that, you'll never hear anything the Lord has to say."

I thought about it as we made our way to our dorm and I knew he was right. Someone once said that God didn't expect us to be sinless, but to start sinning less and I knew that was the truth. "I'll tell him yes. Street Disciples will give me a chance to do something for the Lord and to be able to atone for my sins in some ways."

"Don't do it to atone, do it because you feel the Lord has called this ministry for you."

"I do—besides, I could use Rahliem as a role model."

I felt good about my commitment to Jesus. Some people believed that faith without works is dead and I wasn't going to be standing still doing nothing. I said I was a Christian and therefore, I needed to get on the mission of going out into the world and ministering to His people. I hadn't figured out how I was going to get past the videos I had made or what would happen if a woman from my past confronted me about sleeping with her, but I trusted that God had it under control. After all, with Elicia and Ezekiel by my side, I knew that at least somebody was praying for me.

I Wanna Be Ready

I awakened at 6:30 in the morning and got dressed. As I pulled a solid green sweater vest over the white button up shirt I had just ironed, I felt like the black Doug character on Nickelodeon. The khaki slacks, the black leather Cole Haan penny loafers with my matching black knapsack just added to my character effect. As I looked in the mirror and rubbed my eyes before I put on one of the few luxury items I had for myself, the black wire-rimmed Dolce and Gabbana prescription glasses for my near sightedness. I couldn't figure out why I woke up so early. I didn't even have class this morning. As Kirk Franklin and the Nu Nation Project encouraged me to "Stomp" as the Razr cell phone vibrated and danced on my counter, I realized that the phone call would have eventually woken me up.

"So, we are going to meet at the library tomorrow so we can put my campaign together right?" I looked at the caller ID and couldn't believe that Elicia was this chipper in the morning. I had hoped no one had spiked her drink or given her a bottle of NoDoz. She was hyper enough and excitable without it.

"Yeah, I'm calling my cousin at Bank of America tomorrow so that she can help me find you some sponsors. I'm also calling some of those companies on those party fliers so I can get those prices for you." I had already done all of this work and we had yet to have an official campaign meeting. I had also arranged for Martin Maasai, one of the hottest graphic designers on campus to design us a top notch website with a powerful forum so that Elicia and the team could interact with the students in real time to address any questions, comments and concerns the students had about her campaign. Not only that, we had started to rehearse a couple of songs she'd choose from to sing at the pageant she'd be competing in. Plus, I was pitch hitting on some smaller projects for Gabriella's upcoming campaign, though I didn't have a major role in, was proving to be just as big of an obligation as managing Elicia's whole campaign would be.

"Good, good. I want to make sure that I have everything in order so that I become the next Miss NC Tech. You know that winning is not always about how good you look, but about the best presentation. She who puts on the best campaign is the one who will win. And I want my campaign to be the best."

"Alright, I got you."

Elicia's presence lit up the room, like an aura everyone knew was there. Heads turned in slow motion and synchronized to the hypnotic but organized beat that was played by her walk, her talk and her allusion.

Now I remembered that I agreed to meet her for breakfast at the cafeteria. Before I left the room, I made sure I put on the Egyptian Musk body oil I had gotten from one of the African body vendors who had come on campus the day before. The stuff was strong, probably because I had put on too much. I had been used to wearing colognes before I started developing rashes due to an allergy to one of the ingredients in the cologne. I looked in the mirror to make sure my face was right one more time and I grabbed the new black leather Bible my younger brother had gotten me on his last visit on campus and I was out the door.

***

As Elicia and I left the cafeteria, I didn't know why I sweated this morning's meeting like I was going on a date. Of course, a brother wanted to look good and feel good but I really didn't have a reason to impress Elicia. Once we had eaten breakfast earlier that morning and read a few Bible verses, I came back to my room, took off the slacks, the button up and the vest, put on a pair of basketball shorts and hit the bed. I slept for a little bit and then I studied for an upcoming International Business exam that I had the week of homecoming. Our professor was only giving us three exams and a major project, so getting an "F" was not an option, even though the group project we had with students who were majoring in engineering at A&T accounted for sixty percent of our grade.

Elicia and I met for dinner to hang out, study for our accounting class and to talk about our plans for the campaign. She had changed into a blouse and skirt that was the shade of blue that was one of her sorority's colors.

"You are going to my sorority's coronation later on tonight aren't you? I want to speak to Arnisha *before* the Miss NC Tech University Interest Meeting that will be held three weeks from now and the way our schedules are set now, it will be impossible for me to talk to her before then."

This campaigning business was taking up a lot of my extra time. I'm not complaining because I knew what this job would entail before I took it, but her sorority's coronation had slipped my mind. Homecoming was getting to be too close and the International Business exam, as well as the Business Law quiz was now on my mind. I wasn't stressed but I knew that I was gonna have to pick the studying up a notch with all the commitments that were now on my plate.

"You don't waste no time do you?"

"Boy, I have worked too hard and planned for too long for me to just *lose* the title due to poor planning. I don't give poor performances remember?"

"I know. I'll be there but I will have to meet you at the coronation because I don't get out of class until six o'clock tonight."

"Good, I'll see you there."

"I'll see you there."

I gave her a hug and then I watched her go into the dorm and up the stairs.

The Lord is Blessing Me Right Now

*A*rnez and Ezekiel were sitting at the table with me—working on finalizing the Sickle Cell Anemia service project and working with various study groups for our individual homework assignments. As far as the service project was concerned, most of the SGA executive board was down with the project. All Arnie, who was the SGA Treasurer needed was the figures so we could make sure we had the money in the budget. Our homecoming was the following week, so Arnie and Elicia had been busy working with the concert promoter in making sure that those events were taken care of and that we did not commit money we did not have to the project. Elicia had mentioned that there was a possibility of our SGA making a profit and being able to do more of the service projects many of the executive board members promised to do for the student body when they campaigned for office last year. As we were reviewing some of the plans for the service project that was to be a fundraiser for the Sickle Cell Anemia Foundation, Arnez started crumbling some paper, drawing not only our attention, but those of the students around him that did not have earphones.

"That girl over there with the flower in her hair is checking you." He smiled as he pointed her out. If I didn't know better, I'd figure that he would be interested in the girl.

"What girl?" I looked behind me, but seeing mostly dudes.

"The one on your right."

I looked over and saw Faith. I felt stupid because I did not see her the first time. Our eyes met for a minute and then she went back to reading her book.

"She a'ight. If I wasn't tied down, I'd holla at that," Arnez responded.

"I'm going to talk to her, let's finish this first."

"Dawg," Arnez looked at me with the biggest smile on his face, "go over there and handle your business. We got this."

I shook my head as Arnez waved his fingers to shoo me away as if I were a little kid trying to take an early peak at one of his Christmas presents. Ezekiel chucked and encouraged me to make my move. "Go on."

They were treating me as if I'd never picked up a girl before…I'm sure they knew better but I went along with the program. I got up and grabbed my backpack and I took those few steps that brought me to Faith's table. I could hear "In the Morning" by Mary Mary bumping from her laptop despite the fact that she, too, was wearing earphones. When she looked up, she took off her earphones, "anyone sitting here?"

"Other than you, no."

That was my invitation to sit down and take a seat. I got a good look at the book she was reading and realized it was a tax preparer's study guide. She was working out a problem on one of the tax forms and I saw a bunch of formulas going up and down the page. The directions given looked like she was trying to find the clues to *Where in the World is Carmen Sandiego?* as opposed to solving math problems. I looked at her sheet and the rest of the problems she was working on. "If you are too busy, then let me get your number and we can talk later."

"I'm good," Faith spoke as she put the paper she was working on in the book, "I saw you admiring me dancing and singing."

I felt my muscles lighten up as I smiled. "You had a nice little crowd going."

"I don't do that too often," she admitted. "I was so caught up in my own little world I didn't notice how loud I was until Ms. Simmons came in and busted up my charade. I almost got written up."

"Well you sound nice," I complimented her which made her smile in return. I noticed how light she wore her makeup—simple lip gloss, near skin-tone shade eye shadow and blush. The coco butter she wore left a familiar but light scent.

"Thank you."

Faith and I sat in silence for a few minutes. This wasn't looking too good because it appeared that she had gotten busy with her homework assignment again. *Had I bored her?* I pondered. I wasn't used to working to get a girl. I was used to girls throwing themselves at me. I saw her ruffling some papers and then heard the clatter of the keys being lightly banged on her IBM ThinkPad. Those were the rare laptops that only the honors students were given upon their admittance into the university. I had an earlier version and when word of my "extra-curricular activities" got out, I had to give it back. When I looked up, I saw Elicia and Gabrielle meeting with a few of their sorority sisters. They had grabbed a few party fliers and were passing them out to the students in the library. Gabrielle walked up to our table and handed us a flier, chuckled to herself and walked away. I glanced at the flier and used the opportunity to make small talk.

"There is a poetry slam on Thursday, would you like to go?"

"I'll be performing at the slam. I was getting my act together that I will be performing during the intermission."

"Oh that's what's up." I was a little disappointed because I wanted to take her to the event. I tried to think of another place I could take her to either later that night or during the week. With homecoming fast approaching, I didn't have many options. "We can hook up afterwards," I offered, determined not to give up on the possibility of getting to know Faith better. "We can go to the Living Room Book & Pastry. The sistah that owns the place has a lot of coffees and chais. We can lounge around on the couch and maybe read a good book together."

"Sounds like you got it all figured out," she smiled as she looked up. "Well, can't let a good date go to waste," She said as she was staring at my friends behind me. I turned around and saw my people pointing at me. "I'm assuming that they are going to be there too?"

I knew she knew Aaliyah and Gabrielle, but I pointed out Elicia not knowing how familiar she was to her. "Elicia helps out with NC Tech's SGA. We try to support events that we know students at NC Tech will be participating in."

"Y'all got a lot of unity at NC Tech."

I was surprised she'd insinuate that. Yeah, a lot of us went to NC Tech, A&T, Bennett and other HBCUs because most of us grew up watching *A Different World* or *The Cosby Show* and remembered the profound impact Cosby had on encouraging children to go to school and to experience life at a black university. And not to knock that but it ain't all peaches and cream at NC Tech either. "We got our own drama too, I think what we experience here is no different than what you have going on at A&T."

"And what would you know about that?"

"I'm just saying. We all fell for the Hillman dream."

"Nah, I wouldn't say that. I think that any school, anywhere can be 'Hillman.' It's all about how you choose to make the most of your experience. Yes, I'm a proud Aggie. I work with their Student Union Advisory Board. I spend a good amount of time in the Student Union helping visitors and new students find their way around campus. Everybody knows Faith and it looks like everybody knows you, too!" Faith tilted her head toward a group of students. They were looking at something on their computer screen and then looking at me. One of the girls was being coaxed into walking toward me. As she started walking, another girl at the computer turned up the sound. Everyone in the library could hear one of my videos being played in the background. I was surprised one of the security guards that had been scanning the halls hadn't kicked her out.

"Oh my God, it's really you," the young lady who was star struck walked toward me and shrieked. She wasn't half bad. The sandy brown dyed perm didn't seem to go with her loud low cut shirt and the ripped jeans with the orange and white Nikes that reminded me of an extra from one of TLC's first videos. The girls behind her were giggling and laughing and exchanging high fives. I knew they had put her up to confronting me. As the lady stood at my side, I felt her undressing me with her eyes. I could tell by the look in her eyes that her imagination was fantasizing what it would be like if she and I hooked up together. Too bad she wouldn't get the answer to that question.

"When is your next movie coming out and can I be in it?" she got the courage to ask. When she looked over her shoulder, her friends stopped laughing and seemed to be encouraging her to pursue me. Seemed like while I was chasing Faith, I was being chased myself.

I looked at her and shook my head. "I'm saved. I don't do those movies anymore." I noticed the look of disappointment on her face. "I haven't made those kinds of movies in almost a year."

The young lady looked away from me again in the direction of her peers and then she laughed again. "Come on, stop you lying—put me on. I got more to offer than those broads you have on those videos. Plus, I need some money to go to school. I want to be in a Longstocking video. Get on the *Longstocking*."

If I died and never heard that name again, I'd die a good death. I shook my head and acknowledged her comment. The only way she was getting on *this* "longstocking" would be if I put a ring on her finger. I reached in my bag and pulled out a copy of *The Upper Room* and gave it to her. She looked at the classical style cover depicting a scene from the Bible and scrunched up her nose. If I needed any other confirmation that she wasn't the one for me, the look on her face said it all.

"Does this have pictures?" she appeared annoyed as she flipped through the book and in her over-dramatization, turned the book upside down and started reading the book backwards. I could tell in her mind, she had it mapped out that I was the celebrity that was going to put her on some new stuff—be her break into making feature films, writing books or something like that. When she read the Bible scriptures and seen the stories of people offering their testimonies, she threw the book back at me. "Sorry sucka. How you gonna have all this porn showing that delicious body and all those moves and be about Jesus now?"

"He saved me," I responded proudly as if I had just told my mother I made all A's on my report card. I could feel the Holy Spirit within me thundering with applause. I was proud that I had been given a moment to testify and I did not shy away, denounce or fail to give glory to my savior. God is good.

She, however, was not feeling my praises. I heard her exhale loudly, blowing out air and rolling her eyes. She'd turn her head again and it appeared that she was trying to tell her girls something. When she faced me again, she looked me up and down like she wanted to knock my jaw in. "Whatever."

She stormed away as fast as she came and she took her wrath with her. It was my turn to exhale, but I would not acknowledge her persecution or accept her reject in defeat. I wasn't pursuing her, I was pursuing the woman in front of me that I could tell by her choice of music clearly loved the Lord and Savior. While Faith picked up the daily devotion and began flipping about its not tattered pages the correct way, I heard Patti LaBelle belt out the words to "What A Friend We Have in Jesus." That little reminder made me thankful that the Holy Spirit was still with me.

"Sorry about that," I apologized to Faith for that young lady interrupting our conversation.

"She was rude," Faith noted as she shook her head and watched the girls and her friends pack up and leave, attempting to humiliate me on their way out talking about how "wack" I was. *Sure.* "But I've learned to listen to other people before I speak. I'm glad to know that you are a Christian. I need a Christian man in my life. Where did you get this?"

She lifted up the copy of *The Upper Room* that the rude girl threw at me.

"Ezekiel turned me onto the books shortly after I got saved. There's a lady at Market Street AME that buys the books for the college students who participate in the ministries. I try to keep up with the daily devotions."

"Let me find out you're slipping in your walk." She teased.

"Never that," I replied in confidence. "I do read some of the old Bible stories daily and I'm learning some of the popular Bible verses."

"That's good. That's where your focus should be."

I felt good that Faith was supporting me where I was at in my walk with Christ. Unfortunately, I was used to the negative responses coming from folks when they found out that I don't do adult videos anymore. I'd learn to deal with it and not let it affect me and my work on getting closer to the Lord, but I was not naive enough to believe that Faith or other new people who'd meet me, Donte Speaks, would not be scrutinized for their affiliation with me as it related to my past works. Yet, I was drawn to the fact that Faith got the message that I was a Christian and about the business of serving the Master. However, I knew that I would have to address the movies with her sooner or later. Granted she knew about it before she met me and had told me as much, but she still needed to hear from me. I had hoped to make that conversation happen much later when I got to know her and she got to know me and we decided that "we" had a possibility.

"So we are still on for that get together after the Poetry Slam?" I brought the focus back to the issue at hand before we were rudely interrupted.

"Oh of course, I'm a big girl. I don't let stupid stuff faze me." I loved the way her smile lit up my soul as if she were the sun. I felt the spirit in me growing like a flower in fresh fertile soil and eventually, I smiled back at her. I hadn't had a woman make me feel like that in a long time. I knew I was going to like Faith and that if I played my cards right, I would be in this for the long haul.

"So are you walking back to your dorm alone?"

"Naw, I'm actually here with some friends. They sent me a text letting me know what study room they were in and I'm going to catch a ride with them. But we will see each other after the Poetry Slam."

I smiled as we got up and left table. When I returned to meet up with Arnez and Ezekiel, they were packing up to leave as well.

"Man we can't take you nowhere," Arnez teased.

"I know," Ezekiel jumped in. "Everywhere we go it's Longstocking, Longstocking, Longstocking."

"What you mean?" I defended myself. "That girl was the one being loud and wrong in the library."

"I'm just picking," Arnez confirmed.

"Yeah." Ezekiel continued. "I knew that girl was crazy when I saw her toss that devotion like that. I was hoping that God wouldn't strike her with lightning, playing with his Word like that."

"Maybe she saw a word or a phrase in there that would later on convict her of her actions and realize that she was wrong," I tried not to let them completely trash the young lady. "We never know what words or phrases people latch on to."

"True, true."

When the three of us left the library, we saw Faith and a few of her friends getting into a dark colored van. I couldn't read the writing on the side, but it appeared to be one that belonged to a church. For that, I was grateful to know that she'd be getting home safe...and I had a chance to date a woman that God could have for me.

Rise Up, Sheppard and Follow

*E*zekiel and I set about keeping our appointment to meet Rahliem before homecoming. I had to admit, the more I thought about Street Disciples and Rahliem's vision for the ministry the more I was intrigued. A group of young men gathering together to go out into the world and make disciples as Jesus had commanded us to do —seemed like a way to meet a few brothers in Christ and work on a lifelong project together.

Homecoming week was about to start. Ours was before A&T's, but during those two weeks traffic was atrocious. Everyone from the elders who kept their 1970's and 1980's model cars in top notch shape to the hood cats that had rims on chrome and pimped out rides courtesy of those who wanted to be like Xzibit to the recent grads who had to have the top of the line cars to show off "how well" they wanted us to believe they were doing.

After getting through that traffic jam, we made the hour long journey from campus to the main library in Winston-Salem on the top floor. We had anticipated that the group would be upstairs, possibly occupying a corner that had some desks and chairs clustered together. The older building, which had been around since 1920 had signs of a visible orange carpet and light topaz colored walls that brought to mind one of the *I Dream of Jeanie* television shows. The mini computer lab looked more recent with 1990s feel with several Gateway computers connected to printers in a hub in the middle of the floor. When Ezekiel and I first got on the floor, we didn't see Rahliem or any group of black men congregating. I looked at the time on my phone and knew we were only a few minutes early at the most. I walked to one of the corners I thought the group would be. Not seeing them, I got distracted as I looked outside and stole a glimpse of the BP sign and watched the man raise the price of gas.

"I'm not gonna like that when I get my car next week," Rahliem announced as my heart tried to make its great escape through my chest. I couldn't believe he had snuck up on me like that.

"You think gas will ever go back to $0.99 like it was two years ago?"

Rahliem looked at me like I was crazy and after I thought about what I'd said, I realized he was right. "Nah. We need to pray it don't go up to $2.00 a gallon. That would be crazy." I shook my head in agreement. "We are on the other side—some of the dudes are just getting in though so go ahead relax and get comfortable."

I frowned for a minute and took a peek out of the window. Before I could turn away, I saw this man in baggy black pants and a hockey jersey and a cap hand another man whom appeared to be homeless a package on the sly. I looked at the police officer who was just sitting in the parking lot and was surprised that he didn't notice the action either. I noticed the guy in black look in the direction of the library and then run across the street.

Trying to convince myself that I didn't see what I thought I saw, I followed Rahliem and did as I was told. Ezekiel was talking to a young man who had on an extra long Winston-Salem State T-shirt on and some baggy blue jeans. He was as thin as an anorexic track star but when I shook his hand, I was surprised by how firm his grip was. "Celtius." He invited with a voice that had a deep southern twang that I'd associate with people from Texas. Off bat, I felt cool about Celtius, especially with him being a college student as well. In conversation, he seemed new to the Lord but excited about the journey ahead.

A moment later, we saw a dude who had a fresh perm, and a pencil-thin goatee on his sepia colored soccer player frame. The button up checker shirt he wore had loose threads and jeans that were cut up and should've been thrown in the trash. He looked at us quickly and then looked away, opting to sit at the far end of the furthest desk and chair from the group. Rahliem pretended like he didn't notice the scene and introduced the man casually. "And this is Mya." He stepped closer to the group and whispered, "He's a little shy."

"Hi," he said in a pitch that would make Chris Tucker sound like Barry White. I did a quick look at Rahliem, then had to ask the Lord for forgiveness at the thought that Mya might have been his "prison buddy" if you get what I'm saying. The fact that he waived like a nervous five-year-old school girl only made it harder for me to picture otherwise.

"Come on man—" Rahliem encouraged. "If you were in front of some heathens using Jesus' name in vain, you'd be louder than a broadcaster at a football game."

"Whatever, don't start." I take that back, Mya made had to have had the highest pitch voice of any man I'd ever heard. When he came and sat next to me, I knew something was off...*prison buddy.*

Rahliem scratched his head and I noticed that his cornrows looked freshly greased. Just when he was about to take a seat, in walked a man I'd thought I'd never see.

"Man, if I'd known y'all were coming back home, I would've tried to catch a ride with y'all," Neal Jennings announced in a boisterous voice that caused everyone to turn heads. The fact he had on an A-line T-Shirt, sagging black Dickies that showed off white and black striped boxers, and white ankle socks that were covered by some black clog-style slippers made Neal look like he needed to be in a dorm room or in the privacy of his own bedroom, or on the porch of his mother's house. The elder librarians looked at him with disapproval and shook their heads. I was surprised he wasn't kicked out.

"I didn't know you were coming," Ezekiel defended. I'd caught a ride with him so I definitely didn't know.

"It's cool, I'm here now. We can begin."

"On that note," Rahliem jumped in, taking over the meeting, "We'll go ahead and get started. I've been led to gather you guys together to help me continue Street Disciples and take this ministry to a whole 'nother level."

I looked around and I felt bad for judging, but I didn't see that happening. Mya alone would turn people away between that hairstyle and those mannerisms. Celtius—I couldn't figure the angle out on him. When I looked around and I saw this old lady looking at me and then looking at the computer and then looking at me again, I was reminded of the glass house I lived in, and here I was throwing stones.

"There's a man in Butner named Osiris Street whom I had gotten close with. When time permitted, we read the Bible together and talked about the Lord and ministered to the other inmates. He and I began working with the vision that God placed on our spirits a year before I got out of prison."

I'd never thought that men in prison would be planning ministry programs. I'd heard about people supposedly finding Jesus, Buddha or Mohammed, but I had to admit, seeing the vision to come life brought a smile in my spirit. I knew that I was dealing with the real thing.

"What we saw in the first phase was a tutoring program that would work with the youth ministry like a mentor program where we took young men and taught them everything they needed to know about being a man. In addition to reading the Bible and teaching them sound, faith based principles, we showed these young men how to

shave; how to fix a flat, change the oil and the brake pads
on a car; the correct way to wear a suit and tie; how to read
a map; how the read measurements and follow instructions
in a manual. Basic things a man should be able to do, by
time he's sixteen and thinks he's ready for a car."

I was feeling this. This is what ministry should be about
—not just the preaching of the Bible but showing how we
are living the breathing document through our words and
actions. I could see myself growing into this kind of
ministry.

"Osiris is still locked up until 2010, but in the
meantime, the ministry must go on. I send him letters and
pictures of the different things Street Disciples are doing in
the name of Jesus. I've been working with our pastor and so
far, we got about seven churches in Winston-Salem, two in
Kernersville, four in Greensboro all doing the same thing.
It's good to see different denominations working together
for the common good of saving our boys and keeping them
off the streets.

"Now the second phase is where y'all come in. I want to
put y'all on the streets in some of Winston-Salem and
Greensboro's roughest areas, where the Muslims be at
times, and I want y'all to pass out these books."

Rahliem reached inside the top of his khaki-colored
Dickies and pulled out the pocket size *Upper Room*
magazine.

"So we're giving these away? How are we paying for
them?" Mya's attitude was very flippant with his response.

"Not necessarily. We are taking donations. Whatever the
people want to give us, I'm cool with it, as long as we put
the books in their hands. I'm trusting in the Lord to do the
rest."

"Okay." Mya was doubtful and even though he was a
little annoying at times, I could see where he was going with
it.

"I'm not knocking the idea." Celtius spoke up. He took his hat off and I could see the skull cap he was concealing. "Are we sure we don't have a minimum donation?"

"It would be nice if we got fifty cents per book we gave out but most people are going to give a dollar." Rahliem was very optimistic, like he was the dude who was turning water into wine.

"And there are going to be some people who give nothing," Mya interjected. "I'm not trying to rain on the parade and I think what you are proposing is good. I just don't want us to be taken advantage of. Plus, I'm not trying to be in the middle of the hood wearing suits looking like the fake Nation of Islam."

"We aren't wearing suits. Maybe once or twice—three times a year tops. We are going to wear the latest street fashions. FUBU, ENYCE, Akademiks, whatever style is hot, we are going to rock it. I'm trying to meet the people where they are at."

"I can see this working as long as the members of the church are willing to help finance the ministry so that we can make up a shortfall and stay on the streets," I showed a sign of support. I could see where Rahliem was going with it and all of a sudden, the name Street Disciples was starting to make perfect since to me. We were going to be in the streets giving the unsaved a soft approach to getting the Word.

"You would need to get some glasses and maybe a hat," Mya directed his comment toward me. "Let's face it, everyone on the Tre-4 has seen you naked and a few done did who knows what while they were watching your videos. I'm not hating, but I could see that being a potential problem."

"I have to agree," Celtius jumped in. "But I'd need to wear some glasses and a hat too cause I done been with quite a few people out here."

"Quite a few dudes," Mya mumbled.

"What was that?" Celtius challenged and started to walk over to where Mya was sitting. Ezekiel and I quickly jumped up and met them in the middle. "I don't do that no more and don't you ever bring that up again."

Ezekiel escorted Celtius out of the library to keep him from breaking a foot off into Mya's behind. I looked at Rahliem and I could see he was visibly frustrated. I had to give the man points for trying, but I was struggling to see where everyone was going to mesh together. Speak of the devil, in walks the dude that looked like he was selling drugs a few minutes ago.

"Sorry I'm late Rahliem, I was praying with one of the men when we…" our eyes locked and I knew we were in trouble. I knew dude very well.

"Abednego," I called him out. To keep the peace, I shook the man's hand. Abednego reached for mine hesitantly but he shook it anyway. I didn't like that because I felt like the man was trying to say my hands were dirty or something.

"You still making those videos," the short, stocky, linebacker looking, dark skinned brother with braids that puffed into an afro asked.

"I was in a music video for TLC back in the day," well, that video didn't come out but still, I was in a music video.

"Naw, brother, you know I'm talking about them pornos."

If I could just jump off the top of the building and know that I could still go to heaven I would. Yeah, brother man had already ticked me off this afternoon and he was crawling a nerve a second. Abednego looked at me like I was short or something. Now being the cat from Winston, I could have picked up this chair and started something rough, but I decided that I wasn't going to do that.

"Well brothers, we're here because we are on a mission to spread the Gospel of Christ throughout the city of

Winston-Salem and surrounding areas. We will be handing out pamphlets and copies of devotions at Wal-Mart next Friday. Now Ezekiel, Neal and Donte will be returning to NC Tech tonight we are hoping that they will be able to pass out the devotions on campus for a few weeks to coincide with our efforts here." Rahliem kept talking but I wasn't able to concentrate because I had begun to remember where I met Abednego.

I was filming at this car wash around four o'clock in the morning. The owner didn't know we were using the car wash to do one of my videos. Anyway, I was acting my role when this black Nissan Altima pulls up behind us. I didn't have any shame in my game so I kept doing what I was doing.

"What you doing with my girl?" the man yelled as he was getting out of the car. He hurled some other explicit toward me, Ezekiel and the rest of my crew.

"What are you doing here Abednego?" the girl said.

"What are you doing here with this negro? And you talk about me cheating? This man got you on film and stuff?!"

"You always watching those videos so I felt I would do a video. You always had more time for the women who were just 'holding' your drugs for you, get one of those junkie chicks to take care of you cause Donte is taking care of me."

The conversation got real nasty. Ezekiel had thrown me a towel and my sandals so I could be dressed in case we had come to blows. He threw a fist my way and he landed on my car. I was mad because I had just bought that teal Lexus so I could shoot the video with. I threw a blow to his face and my crew was trying to keep us from fighting. My towel had come off and I caught a blow to my jaw. I was trying to cover my stuff as dude was punching and kicking me. Being on the cold, wet gravel in my birthday suit was one of the most uncomfortable feelings I had ever had. When my crew was finally able to break us up, the police were rolling up on the scene. I knew that would not be a good week for me because my crew had just gotten a citation from the same police officer for doing a scene on top of a seesaw in the middle of Bolton Park. As we all were getting arrested, we tried to fight the police officer trying to get back at each other. We said some very un-Christ like things and threatened to kill each other if we saw one another again.

"I'm feeling some tension between the two of you," Rahliem said looking at both of us. "I feel that as Christians, we should be able to work out our differences. I want harmony in this group and we can't be Street Disciples if we are fighting amongst ourselves. Celtius done already left and I want all of us to defy the odds and show that we can work together so we can get this thing started right."

"It's some stuff that happened before I got saved," Abednego said looking at me. "I think Donte and I need to step outside just the two of us for one minute."

"Cool brothers. Ezekiel, Neal and Mya, y'all hold the table down for a few minutes while I go work with these young brothers."

Abednego, Rahliem and I went downstairs to the parking garage. I felt like I was on my guard because I wasn't looking to fight nobody. For me, even though the incident was fresh in my mind, it did bring a small hint of rage in me. Abednego walked over to his Altima, the same one he had two years ago and leaned against it.

"I didn't know a porno star could be saved," he looked at me and then turned away.

"I didn't know saved people still sold drugs," I retaliated.

My pride was hurt. I was frustrated because it did not seem like I was ever going to be able to shake this porno image that people had of me in their heads. I felt like I was always going to be stuck with it.

"Brothers you got to start from the beginning. Where is all this tension coming from?"

So I let Abednego break down the incident in his own words. He talked about the girl, my video and what they were going through. He mentioned getting arrested and his current probation. As for me, I did a few days in jail and paid a fine for my second offense.

"Well if both of you are saved why is this beef still going on?" Rahliem asked calmly. I couldn't read his body language to tell if he was frustrated or keeping his cool.

"I had forgot about it," I responded. Truthfully, I had until I saw his face and I let my mind take me back down memory lane. "Thought never crossed my mind until I saw him again."

"You didn't see Abednego at the service? He comes to the church frequently."

"Not when I'm there, no. Usually I meet up with Elicia or some of the other college students and we go back to Gilbert together or we go to lunch or something like that."

"That's what's wrong with our churches. We never take the time to welcome the visitors. But that is not what is upsetting. I'm looking at two brothers who I know have a love and admiration for Christ, carry on a street beef that happened before either of you got saved. I say leave the streets in the streets and let us be about God's business. No one is going to try to punch the other person and no one is going to try to kill the other person."

"I'm not trying to do nothing like that. I just wanted to find out what Street Disciples was about since you've been coming to the school and it seems like this is a ministry I want to be part of."

"Cool," Abednego said, "But I do want to clear up something. I wasn't giving that man any drugs. I was handing him a copy of the daily devotion that was in the bag with some other food."

I shook my head and looked at him. He didn't look as mean and hateful as he did when we reintroduced ourselves. I was disappointed because even though we had some mean and negative spirited things to say about one another, I wasn't man enough to put the issue to the side first.

We walked back to the lounge and were able to complete the meeting without incident. As the meeting ended, I pulled Rahliem over to the side to air my grievances.

"I thought that when I got saved, I would be able to live this perfect life and be sinless. What Abednego and I got into was petty to say the least."

"Look," Rahliem confided in me, "everyone makes mistakes—even after they get saved. But I'm going to tell you something that a friend told me after I got out of prison and started my journey with Christ. He doesn't expect us to be sinless, he expects us to start sinning less. Look at you... you used to make a few videos a week from what you telling me. Once you got saved, you don't make any videos at all. You probably don't have sex nowhere near as much as you used to. The thoughts are probably still there and will probably always be there because you will remember what was and there may even be the temptation to go back after you get saved. But the miscellaneous sex with miscellaneous people has ended. You're not following all of the thoughts with the decisions to have sex, right?"

"True."

"Everyone is not going to get it right all the time. That's why Jesus gave his life on the cross because he knew that *I* was going to mess it up every now and then. That is why we have grace and mercy. That's why I can ask for forgiveness. But you can't seek what you don't ask for and you can't enter a door you didn't knock on."

"I feel you."

Rahliem packed his bag and everyone parted their own ways. I was feeling the Street Disciples ministry concept and I hoped that as time passed, Abednego and I could become cool. Celtius and Mya could put their beef to the side and we could become the men Rahliem pictured us to be. They had good programs and ideas for how they want to spread the good news. As I searched through the packet that Rahliem gave to me. Then I ran across the devotion for today:

"Bear with each other and forgive whatever grievances you may have against one another. Forgive as the Lord forgave you. And over all these virtues put on love, which binds them all together in perfect unity. – *Colossians 3:13-14"*

I could roll with that.

Jesus Promised Me a Home Over There – Homecoming

*U*sually, North Carolina Technical University's Homecoming started on a Monday and ended on a Sunday. Mobile game carts could be found outside and inside many of the academic buildings were various card and board games encouraging the students to be physically and mentally fit on Monday. Tuesday was reserved for the comedy show and we always featured local or lesser known comedians with one large headliner. This year, Rickey Smiley was coming and for the first time ever, we sold out all of our tickets. On Wednesday was the two modeling troupes would coordinate a fashion show; usually surrounding a central theme. Unofficially, it was the first of a yearlong battle the two originations held to show who would reign supreme. One of the groups tried to get me to model when I was making videos but I had declined them because my movies were making me money and tying up my commitments. Now that I'm saved, I haven't heard from them. Thursday was the coronation in which many of the student leaders came out in their finest clothes; some even wearing the outfits they wore to their high school proms and we formally presented Miss North Carolina Technical University to the campus and the world. She would wear a high end fashion gown and her show would revolve around a theme so that everyone could coordinate their outfits to match. After her coronation, she would host the school's official formal homecoming party.

Friday would be the National Pan-Hellenic Council step show in which all of the Greek-letter organizations would compete for a $5,000 grand prize given to the top fraternity and sorority step teams. Usually, an exhibition step team would do a show during the middle of the Greek-letter organizations performance and a "special guest" would perform their hit song after all the organizations performed. For our SGA, the event was the largest money maker because the organizations performed for nominal fees and often helped behind the scenes putting the shows together.

At the same time we had the step show, the Alumni Association would host an "old school" concert in which they invited acts from the 1950's to 1980's to perform. Last year, Diana Ross and the Supremes surprised everyone with a special reunion show in which they performed their top hits. Then Diana Ross performed some of her solo hits with members of the Gospel Choir.

Saturday was the big day in which we had our parade at 8 o'clock in the morning. The parade could last for up to two hours and would start on Dudley Street and go up Market Street. Students from all of the universities nearby would watch the floats, the dancers and the singers do their performances in route to the homecoming game. Vendors would line the streets selling food, homecoming and NC Tech-themed merchandise. Independent artists and authors would sell their CDs and books and pass out promotional material and everyone else would visit before, during and after the game to have a good time. The various colleges and universities would open to welcome the alumni and many of the Greek-letter, social and honor societies would host barbecues and cookouts for their alumni members. The football game would usually start at 1 p.m.. After the game (or during the fourth quarter if we were losing really bad), everyone would lounge around, reacquaint with visiting alumni and just have a good time. Of course, a few of us would be found studying because professors were notorious for giving quizzes and exams before, during and right after homecoming festivities—so much so that everyone knew they had some form of examination on Monday so folks came prepared. People started leaving the campus around five or six in preparation for the big R & B and Hip Hop concert.

Sunday would usually end the Homecoming celebration with an early morning breakfast in the cafeteria, followed by a sermon given by a well-known and respected pastor. Our university was private and independent though our founder was a Baptist pastor and educator. After the sermon, different service organizations would gather together to clean up the campus and the surrounding neighborhoods. At the end of the day, there would be a large gospel concert with one major act, our school choir and visiting high school and other church choirs.

Homecoming was big business for the HBCU's in our area because our school brought the city a respectable $10 to $12 million each year and A&T's homecoming, which would either be the week before or the week after ours would net the city between $15 to $20 million. Businesses loved our homecoming celebrations because it allowed for them to support the schools and to make money in celebration of our major events.

When Malachai campaigned for SGA President, he argued that everyone would have a better homecoming experience if the week started on a Sunday as opposed to a Monday. Malachai's other motive was that being a Christian and since majority of the student population attended Protestant-based churches, Homecoming should start with praises, worship and celebration of the Lord, not end with the Lord as an afterthought. It was embarrassing to admit that no matter how big of an act we brought to the Gospel show, that show usually lost money every year and if the R&B and Hip Hop did not do well, our SGA was usually deep in the red. Last year, money was so tight that our executive board voted to suspend their monthly stipends and the president and Miss NC Tech paid for their room and board out of pocket as opposed to it being paid for out of the student tuitions. The SGA also had to ask three of our university's associate chancellors for a $35,000 loan just so SGA could do its service and school based events and be functional.

Ever since Malachai won the election, he and the other members of the executive board fought the administration, leaders of various alumni associations (who had graciously paid half of the loan for us) and our concert promoters to move the Gospel Concert and church service to the Sunday before Homecoming. He even reached out to the nation's religious leaders with surveys and many of them expressed a desire to preach and perform worship services at the start of Homecoming and not after it. Over the summer a well renowned pastor agreed to preach the opening sermon while Kirk Franklin and Richard Smallwood agreed to perform during the service as well as headline this year's gospel concert.

"This was a great decision," Malachai Sharp, the SGA president bragged as he, Arnisha, Donlynne, Arnie, Elicia, Ezekiel, and myself walked to the head of the long line that wrapped around our coliseum to unlock the door and to work the ticket booth for the gospel concert. Everyone smiled and nodded their head in agreement. His fight of faith was a good fight and putting God first showed to be a great victory and would probably lead to us paying back the chancellors of their loan with this concert alone.

When we got to the front of the line, Rahliem, Abednego, Neal and Mya were passing out party fliers for Market Street A.M.E.'s campus sleep-in, which would take place the Sunday after Homecoming. The four guys wore grey hoodies with a big cross on the back that had the words "Jesus Saves" on the back with black baggy jeans and black work boots. Outside of the hoodie, all of them had big, wooden, beaded crosses that they also were selling to raise money for the ministry.

Our Homecoming came before A&T's this year and we could see a large number of their students in line for our Gospel concert. I had taken my spot with a security officer verifying student IDs for our students as well as visiting students from other colleges. One by one, we let the students in the coliseum. As one would expect, there were no issues with either the students or the community members attending. Once I was done helping with admission, I worked with the other members of the Street Disciples Ministry to help man one of the concessions booths.

"Y'all should do the Gospel concert first every year," Rahliem advised as we watched Kirk Franklin's energetic performance on the monitor. I was filling the paper cups with ice while Abednego was fixing the drinks. Neal was at a table about ten feet to the left of our booth selling the crosses some of the volunteers at the church made.

"Yeah man, it feels good starting the year with Jesus first and just by the look at all of the ticket sales, people would rather come to a gospel show first."

"Maybe y'all won't have any issues or incidents this year," Abednego reference the embarrassing fight that happened right after the comedy show last year between the football team and one of the Greek-letter fraternities which had a negative, trickle-down effect on the rest of the Homecoming events.

"I pray not," I responded. "I feel with us beefing up security at all the events and us praying for success and a drama free Homecoming, the Lord will see fit that His will will be done."

"Yeah man, I'm positive about it too," Rahliem jumped in. "I wished that I hadn't done all of that time in Butner and taken my studies in high school more seriously—I'd probably be in school now."

"It's not too late," Abednego jumped in. "I'm going back next year. I got done talking to my lawyer and we found a school here that may let me take some classes on a conditional basis."

I didn't even think about how Abednego's drug conviction and Rahliem's felony assault charges interfered with their ability to pursue higher education—a feat that would be even more difficult if either of them chose to go to seminary school.

"Yup, I'm trying to go to the new Bible School they plan on opening in the next few years in Winston-Salem," Abednego said with enthusiasm.

Kirk Franklin finished ministering to the crowd through his music and his choir doing a surprise performance with Richard Smallwood's choir for their take on his popular "Total Praise" song. I looked out of the booth and saw that Neal had his hands full with people wanting the crosses and soon, we were busy serving drinks and snacks to the concert patrons. It felt good fraternizing and getting to know Rahliem and Abednego on an individual basis. If one had asked me a year ago whether or not the three of us would even co-exist in the same room, the answer would have been a resounding "no." But I felt the Lord's spirit working through us and preparing us for the ministry that was to come.

How I Got Over - A Coronation

After the gospel concert and having our spirits uplifted by TD Jakes, Kirk Franklin and Richard Smallwood, I noticed a very good change on campus. Students seemed to be friendlier on Monday and more joyous as we started the Homecoming festivities. On Monday, our fitness and health awareness seminars and activities went without a hitch and even I became more aware of my health and the foods I was putting into my body. Tuesday, Rickey Smiley did a faith themed show in which he talked about and did imitations of all of our headliners and he even tried to prank Steve Harvey, getting him on the line for a few jokes as well. Wednesday, the two modeling troupes did a *School Daze*-themed fashion show where they re-enacted parts of Spike Lee's popular social commentary film and even performed popular songs such as "Straight and Nappy" and "Da Butt."

As I was preparing to go to the Miss NC Tech coronation, Elicia was in my room, trying to help me pick out an outfit as we went over some campaign proposals. Hanging out with the Rahliem, Abednego, Ezekiel and Mya and working on some Street Disciples projects and studying for the Money and Banking exam I had earlier took up so much of my time, that I didn't think to get a nice suit together for the formal coronation. I knew her theme was "Stealing Away to Freedom" so a suit and tie wasn't too bad. Elicia was wearing a green sweat outfit because she was getting dressed at the coronation. We had finally settled on a dark brown tie, a white button up and a dark brown suit. I had managed to find the pair of dark brown suspenders that went with my tie.

"How does my tie look?" I asked Elicia as I stepped outside my room. I shared a suite with three other students. She was sitting on the couch we shared, reading a Victoria Christopher Murray book that someone had left on the coffee table.

"No one is going to see your tie. Put that on and come on. I need to get there so I can help set up the props."

I had also forgotten that was the reason that she was dressing up at the coliseum. When I wasn't busy with ministry and school, I had been busy working on campaign ideas and going over campaign platforms and ideas in the two weeks since Elicia had made her announcement to her committee. She and I spent a lot of time together working behind the scenes to help put together our school's homecoming. For the concert, we were able to get Nas, Jill Scott, Musiq, Bilal and Michelle Williams for our conscious-themed show and were helping Arnie and Amir Dudley, our vice-president of external affairs and planner of Homecoming, work out last minute details for our special guest. Elicia also spent time with Arnisha behind the scenes working on the theme to her coronation. She had been helping with the recreation of the old slave houses and the woods that were being used as part of the theme. We were getting into the car to drive to the school coliseum to finish setting up props when Elicia's phone had ringed. Her rush and excitement turned into a sad tone. She turned to me and handed me the phone. It was a good thing I hadn't started the car yet.

"Hello."

"Donte, I really need your help," the woman on the other end was sobbing on the other end. She sounded as if someone had been twisting her arm in agony and that the person still wouldn't let go. I had to look at the screen to realize it was Arnisha.

"What's going on?" I questioned because I knew that if she were calling to ask to speak to me, something bad had happened.

"Arnez got into a real bad car accident on the way to school about an hour ago and he's in the emergency room." I registered what she said and I immediately bowed my head and sent a quick prayer for Arnez' healing and for the safety of the others who may have been involved. "He was —I need a dancer. Can you do it?"

In addition to being the parliamentarian of the executive board, Arnez was also a talented dancer and was part one of the modeling troupes on campus. I remembered that he and Arnisha had been working on their routine for a month and I had only seen rehearsals of the performance twice.

"How long do I have to practice?" I was concerned because while the routine did not look difficult, I knew that I still needed to be familiar with the final layout and I didn't know all the steps to the dance moves they, along with everyone else who was in the coronation had been practicing.

"Thirty minutes, and it will only be with a stand in."

Thirty minutes was dangerously cutting it. When I used to do videos, the "actresses" and I even spent two hours rehearsing our script and going over what they wanted/ didn't want in a scene. This was for Homecoming and the last thing I wanted to do was mess up and the whole school be mad at me. Of course, I didn't tell her that. "Alright, I can do that."

Arnisha said thank you about a thousand times before she hung up. I told Elicia that I was going to be in the coronation and she smiled. I couldn't believe I had agreed to be in this coronation in a lead role at the last minute because usually, I turned down requests to perform at the last minute—especially if I hadn't conditioned in a while.

"Don't worry about the people. You will be okay," Elicia spoke as if she had read my mind. Even though she didn't agree with the movies I was making, she was still privy to all the conditioning and some of the things I had done to "practice" for the roles I used to do. I started the car again and made the way to the coliseum. I had said "yes" moreso on the spur of the moment than thinking it through. Thankfully for us, we met with Malachai as he was driving to the coliseum. He already had a heads up on the situation and instructed me to ride with him back to the housing unit our suite was in. He also told me that it would give him an opportunity to change into his costume as well. When we got to his suite, he went over some of the dance routine with me because he knew that some of the others who were participating in the coronation still had not arrived at the coliseum yet and they would be briefed on Arnez' condition as a group. I had gotten the basics down but I still needed to practice some more.

When Malachai was done changing, I rode with him to the coliseum. Malachai split while Elicia was rushing to a door the designated for the decorating committee. Mary and Ezekiel saw me and immediately escorted me to the room some of the dancers were rehearsing in. Upon my arrival, I was ordered to strip down to my boxer briefs so that the design team could come up with an outfit for me while I rehearsed. Most of the other dancers and class representatives were already in costume. Mary had another girl stand in for her while she played Arnisha's role. As I practiced with Mary, many of the tips Malachai gave me came to mind. After a while, I had forgotten that I had very little clothes on and it helped that everyone was so into making sure that they were into their performance, that no one really noticed what I wasn't wearing.

When our rehearsal was over, it was time for everyone to line up and get into position. We had thirty minutes before the coronation was about to begin and I was given a pair of raggedy pants and Arnez' dingy and tattered shirt that was cut up to match the pants to wear. Arnisha met with me and gave me a great big hug. She and I found a little time to go over our dance routine together while we were in line. I felt confident going over the routine with her and my nervousness dissipated. We could hear the old Negro spirituals being sung by our school's gospel choir and I could hear Arnisha humming the words to herself. I was excited because no one knew that I was performing.

Malachai could be heard quoting scripture and preaching a sermon talking about the importance of a man and a woman staying together during times of trial. As Arnisha and I began to make our move to the gym floor, we saw various representatives of the organizations on campus opening the ceremony with hand claps and foot stomping as they sang along with the choir some of the hymns recreating the outdoors religious ceremonies the slaves had during that time period. Each organization's king and queen was announced as their choreographed dance led them to the center of the stage and off dancing into the sidelines.

Arnisha and I split up so we could begin to play our roles. The tone of the coronation had changed from jubilant to suspenseful as one of Arnisha's attendants who was playing Harriet Tubman appeared in the middle of the gymnasium. She ordered everyone to hush that racket so that the slave chasers wouldn't hear them. She did a role call announcing the class officers and royal court as they started moving throughout the fake trees and into a wooded area that had them on stage. Meanwhile, Arnisha and I could be spotted being chased by some slave catchers. Once all of the officers and attendants were all accounted for, the attendant playing Harriet Tubman came and got us and led us to the center of the stage. I was led on stage under my real name, which was a surprise since Arnez' name was on the printed program.

When Arnisha was introduced, the whole audience stood on their feet and clapped. The attendant playing Harriet Tubman led her to meet me at the center of the stage and Malachai came out and continued his sermon as Arnisha and I played the happy couple getting married. Once we were pronounced husband and wife, we shared a playful kiss and we jumped the broom and ran down the aisle heading toward the reception. Once our routine was over, she was led back into the coliseum before the students where she spoke a few words about the importance of brothers and sisters sticking together throughout good times and bad times and she was serenaded by a man singing "Wade in the Water."

Once the show was over, Arnisha was taking pictures with various members of the executive board. Arnisha grabbed me for a few photos and we continued to play the husband and wife role in some of the shots. I saw some of the students watching us as the cameras were flashing and I was waiting on someone to say something about me being in the pictures. Elicia and Mary were off to the side talking and hanging out with other members of the royal court. Once we were done taking pictures, we walked across the street to the Student Union into a ballroom where the reception was held. I sat with Arnisha in the spot reserved for Arnez.

"Are you nervous?" Arnisha whispered as I helped her into her seat.

"A little. This turned out to be really nice," I was amazed as I looked into the crowd. I couldn't believe the ballroom was packed from wall to wall with student leaders, faculty and administrators.

"Well, you performed exceptionally well in the coronation considering you only had thirty minutes to learn the routine. Look at the audience," I looked as Malachai made a toast to Arnisha. We lifted our glasses as some people took a sip of the Fresca and punch. Others were talking amongst themselves. "You are an intelligent brother and a saved man of God. If I thought any less of you than that, I wouldn't have had Elicia to have you come. Besides, this is *my* coronation and if I say you belong, you belong."

I thought about what Arnisha was saying as she got up to thank folks for putting the show together. We also were briefed about Arnez's condition, and we were pleased to hear that he would be coming back to school in two weeks. I saw Elicia sitting with Aaliyah and Gabrielle at a table closer to the center of the room. She smiled at me and I smiled back. Aaliyah was grilling someone in my direction. I looked to my left and I would see Donlynne returning the grill. When Donlynne saw me looking at her, she dropped the frown for a smile. It was terrible to see them acting like that at the coronation. We got up to get our food and Ezekiel came up to me.

"I was surprised to see you on stage. I didn't know you could dance."

I looked at him and started laughing, "Man don't even come up here and tell me that lie."

"I was surprised that she picked you. That's all. I had heard rumblings about you being a last minute addition but I didn't know you were stepping into Arnez' place though."

"Me too, but this isn't about me, it's about her. Most of those people hadn't said anything about me. I thought it would be a big deal for me to be in the coronation."

Ezekiel chuckled then he patted my back. "Naw, Arnisha straight got in everyone's behind about them saying anything about you replacing Arnez. For a minute, I thought she wasn't saved."

I was laughing because I could picture Arnisha going off on everyone. From what I had heard, she's been going off on someone every day since they started rehearsing for the coronation. Now in her defense being Miss NC Tech can be stressful, especially during homecoming. She's got a vision she has to make sure was implemented to perfection. She planned the reception for coronation and sponsors the luncheon for all past Miss NC Techs. She also put together the program for the ladies interested in being Miss NC Tech in the next few weeks. Not to mention the time she spent talking to each hopeful who approached her during homecoming to state their interest.

"Arnisha will be fine. She's a good woman," I defended her.

"That is true."

I went to sit with Arnisha at the front of the table and I tried to picture what it would be like if Elicia were up here instead. As I continued to mingle with Arnisha and the rest of the students, I decided it would be nice.

O Perfect Love

*H*omecoming came and went by so fast after the coronation. During the step show performance, Virginia based rap group The Clipse surprised everyone by giving an impromptu concert performing their hit single. During the parade the following day, I rode the float sitting next to Arnisha with the other members of the executive board. We watched as our football team beat Virginia Union and as a surprise to many, Missy Elliot performed her current hit single before Musiq Soulchild hit the stage.

The following week was the Poetry Slam that Faith and I had talked about. Faith performed with several students from Gilbert, A&T, Bennett, UNCG and other surrounding schools. Most of the poems were about school, sex and the opposite sex. There was a mixture of new and experienced poets flexing their skills on the mic. The intermission came and to my surprise, Mary and Arnie sang "Ain't Nothing Like the Real Thing," by Marvin Gaye and Tami Terrell. The neo soul-like version definitely hit a spot. Next up, this pretty young thing from Bennett sang a version of "Brown Skin" by India.Aire that was reminiscent of Millie Ripperton. A little sped up but cool nevertheless. Then Faith got on stage wearing a preachers robe and her background singers were fanning themselves as they took their seats in the front row.

"Before I begin, I want everyone to turn to Proverbs 17:17. We are going to talk about friends. Now the Bible says 'a friend loves at all times, and kinsfolk are born to share adversity.' A friend is going to be with you through thick and thin. And when I think about a friend, I think of someone who is going to carry me when I get weak. I think of someone who does not judge me for my past but treasures me for what I have to offer in the present. A friend that is going to have my back, not talk about me behind my back."

"Amen!" her background singers said as they jumped up and continued with their church scene.

"One of the important things I feel," That was when the instrumental came on, "I want a friend to pray for me, pray with me and for others. And I want to let the special man who came to see me today know, that I'm saying a prayer for you."

"I say a little prayer for you," the background singers bowed their heads and closed their hands. I was amazed at the religious aspects they brought to the performance of the Aretha Franklin classic. Faith kept looking at me as she sang. Her voice blended in with the harmony with the keyboard and drums. Everyone was clapping and singing along with Faith. I had never been sung to before and I bet I was blushing. Fortunately, no one could see me with the room dimmed, even with the candles burning bright. When Faith and her girls finished their number, they received a booming applause. Faith ran over to me and gave me a hug.

***

I surprised Faith and picked her up at her dorm. I took her to Grace United Methodist Church and introduced her to my pastor and some of the elders in the church. I was nervous because I had never taken a female to church before. We received numerous compliments on how good we looked together. I then took her around the mall, window shopping and enjoying each other's company.

"We look like an old couple," Faith was holding on to my arm, leaning her head on my shoulders, "walking around, taking in the sights."

"We're not old."

"I didn't say that," she said walking around, taking a note of all the women who have been lusting after me, "I do need to let these women know that you are my man."

We walked into the Ruby Tuesdays. The waiter escorted us to a seat in the back of the restaurant. The place was dark but the music was soft. After we finished our meal, Jill Scott came on to talk about her "Long Walk."

"I love this song," Faith commented as she started singing along with the words.

"The song's okay, but there are two things she says in this song that I can't get down with."

An expression of surprise lifted itself on to Faith's face, "What's that?"

"First, I like to keep all references to God in the Bible," I say. When I saw Faith nod her head, I continued, "secondly, I can't smoke no trees. I can drink some leaves baby."

"I never paid attention to that—I like the melody in the song but I see what you are saying," Faith replied. Then she sings, "we can see a play on Saturday, or maybe we can drink some leaves…okay, I can do that. Drink some leaves, that's cool, I love to drink some leaves, too."

We finished our meal and left the mall. As we rode back to Greensboro, the trip was silent, except for the music playing on 97.1 WQMG. Jill Scott came on again, talking about the way he loves her. We look at each other and held hands for the rest of the ride. We ended up at the Living Room Book & Pastry, a local bookstore close to the school. As we walked in we could smell the cinnamon incense burning in the background.

"Welcome to the Living Room Book & Pastry," the sales clerk shook my hand, "I know you from somewhere."

"I've been on film," I replied. I wasn't trying to be mean but that was all he needed to know. I could tell the brother was friendly and meant no harm by it.

"Well, our books are buy four get the fifth free and we have a deal on some cheesecake and other desserts."

Faith had followed the salesman to the cheesecakes while I looked around the store to see which books I was going to read. I walked over to the local authors section and picked up the book. I looked at the back cover and saw a picture of a man who looked like the salesman on the back cover. I looked at him again and seen Faith making her way to the living room area.

"Jaeyel?" I asked.

"That's me," the salesman replied. The name sounded familiar but I couldn't quite put my finger on it. Then I remembered and as I thumbed through the pages of the book, I remembered where I knew him from and most importantly, how he knew me. Jaeyel had sent my production firm a copy of this book I was holding, which at the time had a cheap looking cover on it and a script and was trying to sell the movie rights to the book to me. I'm not gonna lie, I was feeling the book and had even considered doing the deal, but I knew I didn't have the money to do the movie right so I said no. I felt bad then because I didn't even buy his book.

"You sell a lot of copies out this store?" I inquired.

"Yep. Everyday the store opens I got a book to sell. Best place for me to sell the book because every time a customer comes into the store I have an opportunity to market myself and get my name out there. No one comes into this store without being offered a copy of my book."

"Sounds like me. I bet you got a case full of those books in your car."

"Of course, it's everywhere I want to be."

I laughed a little as I had him autograph a copy of the book for me. I was going to pay for this book. I knew the book wasn't a Christian title but I believed in supporting black men my age who were about business. The fact that I knew he was still studying at A&T was a plus. Being a young black male entrepreneur and managing my own entertainment firm, I knew it was hard to promote your self-published art, especially if you were going to college full time. I remembered selling my videos out of the trunk of my car. I would catch people at gas stations, beauty salons, barbershops, concerts and strip clubs. I was even bold enough to go to the daycares, write my name and number on some of the bathroom walls across town and catch a few people after church. I was bad, but I remember the struggle to build my name so I could get my tapes out there. I also took the opportunity to give him a copy of the *In Touch* devotional that I had in the binder I carried with me in the store. Hopefully I planted a seed somewhere because I didn't know if he was saved or not.

After I paid for the book, I walked over to the living room section and sat next to Faith. I took the cheesecake from her and started feeding her. Faith laughed and giggled because she never had anyone do that for her before. She kicked off her shoes and started to lay her head in my lap. She almost got too comfortable as she looked up in my eyes. In this moment, I saw a woman who was feeling me for me. Faith wanted to sip some tea so she got up from her spot.

"I should tell you about my videos." I wanted to be able to talk to her on my terms. Not being bamboozled by a crazy fan obsessed with who I was.

"Oh," Faith coughed and squeezed her cheeks in. I guess the tea burned her tongue.

"My bad."

"No, it's not you. I knew about the videos. The roommate I was staying with two years ago used to have your calendar. And she used to watch your videos all the time."

"Wow—so it doesn't bother you?"

"If it bothered me I wouldn't be here. If anything, I didn't think you could roll with a size twenty sistah like me. You always had those skinny women in your videos."

I laughed a bit, "I made a few videos with some healthy sistahs. They may not be the most popular in the collection but they do exist. One thing I can say is that I didn't discriminate. I mostly did videos with black women. That was my fan base."

"You don't talk about your videos a lot."

"At first I didn't, but as I got older and stronger in my faith, I have learned how to be honest about who I used to be. In my honesty, I can minister to others because instead of condemning those who seek my counsel, I can tell them from experience about how to avoid the pitfalls. Even in all the bad I had done, He has found a way to use it for my good."

"What was it like though, living the fantasy?"

"Suicide."

"Why'd you say that?"

"I was performing with multiple women every two to three days. The first few shoots were cool. The money wasn't what I thought it would be at first, but at the same time, it was easy. Once I learned how to handle my business behind the scenes and gain better control of my product, I found a way to make the videos work better for me.

I loved the business and the respect that came with being a young black man in the industry trying to do my thing. There weren't a lot of black people or young guys who owned their own images and production companies. Being in the industry helped thicken my skin and showed me how to develop relationships that would serve their purpose either at the moment or later on.

I used to love performing, but after a while, some of the people I started performing with began to get pulled in God's direction. I hated that because I felt like he was taking all of my friends away from me. Then they would come to the shoots or when we were on our breaks and start talking about Jesus to me. As I was getting with different women, I started feeling empty. Every time I would get with a lady, I would feel good for that duration of time, and then I would feel like a piece of me would get up and walk away when it was over. Then I started having these dreams about going to Hell and that I was leading folks there. I couldn't take it no more so I asked Him to make the nightmares go away."

Faith took all this in as she finished eating her cheesecake. I anxiously awaited her reaction to find out if judgment day was coming for me.

"I didn't always accept being a big, beautiful woman. I always tried to diet and exercise and starve myself just to make myself thin. I wanted so much to look like Tyra Banks or Aaliyah instead of embracing the beauty of full-figured women like Star Jones, Queen Latifah or Kelly Price.

"I wanted to be thin so badly, I would buy elegant dresses in size ten or twelve, praying I would fit into them. I bought the Tae-Bo, Richard Simmons, paid for personal trainers—I tried everything. I hated myself so bad that I would blow up pictures of myself and write 'I HATE YOU' in red lipstick.

"One day I had enough. I went through my mom's medicine cabinet and took a pill out of each container. I mixed some whiskey and some gin and poured a little detergent in the glass and I swallowed the pills and drank the mixture. I just knew from the chemistry class and the internet that I mixed the right amount of pills together to make for a painless death.

"I was disappointed when I woke up at Moses Cone. My mother sat there crying at my side. I was so mad at God, that He was sparing my life. She turned on the television and I saw Mo'Nique doing standup. She was doing a segment on being proud to be a big black woman. She talked about her growing up and embracing being a big girl. From there I would begin to love myself and love God. I started to lose some weight. Not a lot, but I'm not a size twenty-eight anymore. I'm comfortable as a size twenty. Trying to lose weight isn't a priority anymore."

The light went off, signaling that it was time for the store to close. Faith and I went to the register so we could pay for some books that Faith had picked out. Once we finished, we drove back to A&T so I could drop her off. I have never told anyone how I felt about my life in the industry and the tugging and pulling the sleeping around was doing with my spirit. I was like being addicted to a drug. That first high was the good high and then after a while, you were always trying to chase and recapture that first feeling.

"I enjoyed spending the day with you," Faith said.

"Me too."

"We're going to have to do it again."

She shouldn't have said that. I felt like I had a dog in my lap that would not follow directions. Fortunately, it was a little dark but even then, I was hoping she didn't notice. I haven't done that in a while and that reminder was all I needed to go buck wild.

"We'll get together another time," I responded. I exhaled as my nonverbal commands to cease and desist were being obeyed. For a minute there, I thought I was going to fail and make her an offer that could put our newfound relationship in jeopardy.

We Won't Leave Here How We Came

*T*had given Elicia a ride home for the weekend. She was going to pick up some hair, skin, glamour and spa products that some of the students had ordered. Under her mother's supervision, Elicia sold M.Walker Products door to door, also giving out the Word to anyone who would open their doors to her. We made these trips weekly sometimes twice a week as students would order more products.

Mrs. Edmonds was outside getting the decorations for Christmas together on the lawn when we pulled up. I loved watching her move the Nativity scene as it always displayed the real reason for the season. Oftentimes, cars would pull up and take pictures of the scene featuring characters of color in front of her house. I helped Elicia get settled and made sure she had her things together and then I went to see Mrs. Edmonds.

"Mrs. Edmonds," I yelled so I wouldn't scare her. She turned around and she dropped the lights she had in her hand.

"Hey there, Donte," she gave me a long hug and a kiss on the cheek like the ones grandmothers give their grandchildren, "I'm glad you came. I take it Elicia is inside?"

"Yes ma'am. I can finish this work for you."

"No, an old lady will be fine. Besides, I'm almost finished anyway."

"Are you sure, it won't hurt me to do it?"

Mrs. Edmonds gave me the prettiest smile, so I knew not to argue. I went inside and I fixed both of them a drink and I met Elicia in the living room. I looked at the picture of an older angel that was hanging over the couch. It seemed as if every time I looked at it, the angel would move, or smile. She was beautiful. I sat down next to Elicia at the table. Mrs. Edmonds came in and she sat at the table next to us. Elicia filled her in on what was going on at the church and on how her clients were doing. Mrs. Edmonds, in turn let her know how things were going in church and how her oldest brother, Everett was doing.

Mrs. Edmonds and Elicia got up and I followed them to a closet in the hallway. Looking at all of the products on the shelf reminded me of a small store fronts with the tags on the railing and the small boxes on the side of the hallway, presumably to replace some of the products on some of the bare shelves. Mrs. Edmonds gave me some bags and we started packing some of the orders from Elicia's customers. Once the orders were filled, I was given a big empty box to put everyone's orders in and when we were finished, we went back into the kitchen.

"So how is the campaign going?" Mrs. Edmonds asked.

"Everything is going fine mom," Elicia said, "I feel that I have a good chance of winning."

"Winning is good, make sure you don't compromise your principles to do so…you too, Donte."

"Yes ma'am."

"You are going to have many trials and tribulations and a lot of things about a lot of people will be revealed to you in this election. I should know," Mrs. Edmonds was speaking about Everett's current term as Vice President of the SGA at Shaw University. I remembered hearing the stories of how ugly the campaign had been—to the point to where some of the student leaders weren't speaking anymore and that the campus was more divided. Freshman year at NC Tech was like that too—especially since two former best friends ran for president. "But in all the trials and tribulations is the true test of your faith. Sometimes, it's not about whether you win or lose because the real battle isn't yours, it's the Lord's."

All of that sounded nice, but I didn't expect there to be a clean race. I knew enough about business deals to know that in order to win, opponents were liable to do and say anything. That was my caution about being selected to being Elicia's campaign manager. I didn't want to face my videos or the pictures I'd taken for some adult magazines every time I turned around. I wanted the focus to be on the issues and Elicia's platform, but I knew that being in this role, that would not be the case. I would have to trust God that's he'd use this as a lesson for me later on in life.

"My daughter told me you were surprised that she selected you to be her campaign manager. Why is that?"

Mrs. Edmonds always had faith in me that was one of the reasons we got along so well despite how things may have played out between her daughter and I. Other than my parents, I knew I could trust her with just about anything. I looked at the portrait of her son that was hanging from the wall that was noticeable from where I was sitting and looked back at her. "People won't see Elicia if they got their minds on me."

"Well, you let Elicia worry about her image and making sure that *she* is the center point of her campaign. You worry about making sure the business end is on point and you will be fine." I smiled, but Mrs. Edmonds had known me for twelve years. She knew this wasn't a smile. "I tell you what your problem is. You are worried too much about your past. You don't need to worry about the movies, but focus on what you are doing now after the videos. You have done a lot to turn your life around and your life is turning around. When you gave your life to Jesus, He forgave you of your sins. You need to forgive yourself."

"I have."

Mrs. Edmonds didn't look convinced. She took a sip from her drink and then placed the cup down. "Well quit reminding Him of what you did and be *thankful* for what He did."

Mrs. Edmonds smiled and gave me a hug. She was right and she got to the heart of the matter. I had forgiven myself but I wasn't appreciative of what He had done for me. But I guess a lot of people are like that. They go on living their lives trying to punish themselves for things they had done wrong. They miss out on happiness and that peace of mind that comes with forgiveness.

We stayed for dinner and Mrs. Edmonds packed us some plates so that we could take our food with us. This beat eating cafeteria food all the time or being stuck eating the pre-packed dry soups all the time. We gave her hugs and loaded everything in the back seat of my car. Now my trunk wouldn't open so we didn't have that room to work with.

As we headed back to campus, the ride seemed slow as I began to let my mind wander and those dreamy eyes of mine let go of what was holding me back. I looked at Elicia and a part of me wished we were a few years younger and that I had made different decisions during our youth. But I couldn't live in the past, I had to learn to move on so that our future could be better.

Wholy, Holy

I had agreed to meet with Rahliem at the bus station to hang out with him. He had gone to Butner to visit with Osiris and to visit with his family. I knew that Butner was a ways from Winston-Salem and with him being a former inmate, they gave him a hard time-trying to break him of the vows he'd made to Jesus.

I almost didn't make it to the bus station as my car was sputtering and had run out of gas right before I could get to Market Street. I tried to turn on my blinkers but only my right light would blink. I shook my head because I knew that this car wasn't going to make it to the end of this semester. I didn't want to, but I knew that I was going to have to get a new car soon. At fifteen years old and over 150,000 miles, the car had run its course. Fortunately for me, some of the guys from Gilbert were driving by and they helped me push the car to the side of the road so it wouldn't be in the middle of traffic. They also gave me a ride to the nearby gas station where I not only had to buy a new gas container to replace the one that was locked I the trunk, I had to get two gallons of gas so that I could get to the station on my own and fill up.

Once I did that, I caught Rahliem getting off the bus. His hair was parted down the middle and blew lightly as the breeze began to pick up. He looked like one of those burglar alarm salesmen with his white button up and solid black tie that was clamped down with a tie-clip. His black dress pants and some shine to them that also highlighted the polish of his new dress shoes.

I'd gotten out of the car to open the passenger door so that I could let him in. I could smell the sandalwood oil he had on before he was ten feet within my door. We greeted with a manly grip and then we got in the car.

"So how was the trip?"

Rahliem looked at me and then he shook his head. "Osiris needs prayer. He's letting some of them correctional officers and the other inmates wear on his spirit and planting the seeds of doubt." I knew that Rahliem was trying not to vent his frustration toward me or the situation but it was written all over his face. "Sometimes, I don't think he understands that I need him to hang in there while we do our thing out here. So he can have a ministry to come home to and begin work."

Rahliem had already made plans to go back to Winston-Salem with Ezekiel so I chose to bring him to the Living Room Book and Pastry. I knew Jaeyel would be working and we'd be able to get some things done ministry wise. When we arrived, we could see Jaeyel politicking with one of the older guys from the neighborhood. I was surprised he wasn't inside the store pushing his book or working the café.

"Jaeyel, what's going on?" I called out to him when I thought there was a break between his conversation and the old man's.

Jaeyel got up and introduced the old man to us and we all shook hands and got acquainted. The old man wore an ankh around his neck and had on a traditional West African garb and a dashiki. Jaeyel had taken two puffs of the marijuana-laced blunt he was smoking and passed it back to the old man. The three shades of red FUBU sweater hung loose from his pencil frame, yet contrasted with the baby blue jeans and the buttermilk colored Timberlands he was wearing. When he exhaled, the unmistakable thin line of smoke caused by the laced joint escaped. "Nothing much man. I was hanging out with the old man for a little while, listening to his wisdom."

Rahliem had taken a seat on the other side of the man on the stoop. I had chosen to remain standing. "Is that right?"

To my surprise, Rahliem reached for the blunt from the old man and took a few puffs and passed it back.

"I was telling the brother about how hard he was going to have to work to maintain a business for himself and how he was going to have to let go of some of these vices," The older man spoke. His voice was deep and rich like James Earl Jones. "I meant to take this from him." He took the blunt and took a few more puffs on it and passed it to Jaeyel. "But I ended up getting caught in the circle. And that's how sin works my brothers. It's a never ending circle that keeps man looking to himself for his solutions instead of calling on the Most High."

"When you say Most High, who are you referring to?" Rahliem asked, declining his turn in the hood ritual for the moment.

"Jesus, who else?" the old man replied. "The Father, the Son and the Holy Spirit. I figured out why men hardly ever ask anyone for help—you want a puff young blood?"

I got caught off guard when he offered me to partake in their earthly pleasure. I shook my head, "I'd choke."

I tried it one time and almost strangled to death. Everyone was enjoying themselves one evening and I had wanted to get some but by time I exhaled, I felt like the air constricting my breathing flow and the next thing I knew I was fighting for air.

"But like I was saying, men don't ask for help because we want to be like God, do everything ourselves. Tell me something, can you name a passage in the Bible where God ever asked any of us to help him do something?" And before any of us could reply, the man answered his own question. "None. Jesus asked all the questions. God never asked man to do anything to help Him. He's told us to do things that were good for us, but never asked us to help him do anything. We call God the Father and most of us want to be like our father so we feel that if He can do anything, we can do anything too. But we forget one important thing."

"What's that?" Jaeyel inquired.

"God created us—we didn't create Him. We'd like to think we can put Him in a box but we can't. We put ourselves into situations and expect Him to pull us out like He doesn't have six billion other souls to worry about."

"But I thought God made us like Him?" Jaeyel questioned.

"No, son, God made us in *His* image—there's a difference. If you read the Bible more, you'd know that. Well, young blood, I got to go. Keep selling those books and if you keep reading that small magazine you were showing me and get you a Bible—probably got one in that store you working in—everything will be alright."

We watched as the man got up and walked to catch the bus near the corner of Market Street and Dudley. I felt good knowing that at least one person was reading a copy of *The Upper Room* that I was passing out. My efforts were not in vain. Jaeyel took a few more puffs of the blunt before he put it out and wrapped it in the paper he'd pulled out of his pocket and put it back where he got in from. He led us into the store which was surprisingly empty. As I turned to the far right wall, I could see the Bibles and a few of other religious books that I'd never noticed before.

"So you're thinking about becoming saved?" Rahliem asked.

"I always thought I could wait until I was in my forties or fifties to do that—" an explicative almost fell from his lips. "My bad—stuff. I'm about to be twenty one in a few weeks, I'm trying to enjoy a few more things before I totally give it up to him."

"What makes you think you gonna see twenty one? We might not see 2003. Jesus will come anytime God the Father gets ready to send him." Rahliem picked up one of the Christian fiction books and then looked for another one. "The Bible says even Jesus don't know when He's coming back."

I had to admit that was true. In my readings of Revelation—well, the few times I tried to read it—I do remember it saying that no man knows the day or the hour. So no minute on this earth was promised to us.

"So what's stopping you from getting saved?" Rahliem was blunt as he approached the counter.

"Myself," I heard the man mumble. I had to admit that was the most honest answer to that question I'd ever heard anyone give.

"Look, to be honest, it don't take but a few seconds to ask the Lord to come into your life. Acknowledge that you do wrong and then get you a Bible and go to a Bible-based church and will learn more about your salvation. It's not as complicated as people look."

Watching Rahliem go to work put me on notice. I understood how and why people gravitated to him and why he was able to lead such a ministry.

"Do you accept Jesus Christ as your Lord and Savior?" Rahliem looked him dead in the eye and challenged him to say anything different.

"I'm willing to."

"Do you admit that you are a sinner and willing to ask the Lord to forgive you of your sins?"

"Yes!" I heard him whimper. I didn't notice it before, I but I saw Rahliem's arm outreached and the palm of his hand on Jaeyel's head. I saw Jaeyel's body tremble and rattle like a maraca. "Lord, please come into my life."

And just like that, Rahliem let him go and a calm appeared over Jaeyel. Rahliem nodded and shook his head. "That wasn't so bad."

"No," Jaeyel answered a short while later.

"Take this book, read it with that *Upper Room* you were given, go to that church across the street when they have service and you will be alright."

Jaeyel picked up the fiction novels that Rahliem had placed on the counter and rang up his order. I knew from that moment on that he would never be the same again. Once the transaction was finished, I followed Rahliem outside.

"Man, I thought we'd be able to sit down and talk a little bit more." I wasn't complaining but I did throw that comment out there.

"God had different plans. I was being obedient to them." I couldn't disagree with that. We walked to my car. I had to jiggle the handle up and down a certain way to open the door for Rahliem. I did that so that he wouldn't accidentally make the handle come off as Ezekiel had done once before. Then I ran to my side and started the engine. "It's okay to have nice things, it's not okay to put the material things above others, know what I mean?"

I nodded my head because I knew exactly what Rahliem was trying to say.

Count Your Blessings

*E*lite, Inc was a nonprofit leadership organization designed to help female student organization presidents and officers at NC Tech became more effective leaders and be more visible in the school community. The ladies met once a month for a luncheon and to exchange ideas on how to make themselves stronger leaders. Elicia served as president of the club.

"Donlynne and Monica got into it at the meeting," Elicia told me as I was walking with her. I had come from an accounting study group from the library so that I could get a better understanding of what was going on in that class. I was doing okay, but I didn't want to fall behind either.

"What happened? Which Monica?"

All these girls named Monica on this campus, I was going to need for Elicia to be more specific.

"You know Monica Freeman?"

"You're talking about that girl who can sing? The one that was at y'all's coming out show talking about blacks aren't Greek?"

"Yeah that was her," Elicia exhaled as she relived the show and the embarrassment that Monica had caused them, "well, Donlynne had asked Elite to endorse her campaign to be Miss NC Tech."

I knew that was trouble. From what I gathered, all the women who were somebody on campus were in Elite and I figured that organization to be the one organization all of Elicia's future competitors would have in common. "Isn't Mary in Elite, too?"

"Yeah. She and I didn't say anything. Donlynne announced that she planned to run and Monica cut her off reminding her that she's not supposed to be soliciting endorsements until February. Donlynne went on about how she was just announcing that she was running and Monica said she was running too but didn't expect Elite to endorse her."

"Monica's gonna run for real?" That was a shock to me. Monica didn't seem to be the type of woman who would run for Miss NC Tech.

"We'll see. Personally, I think Donlynne was just trying to find out who was running. I know Mary has told her team not to say anything and my team isn't going to say anything. If Donlynne knows I'm running then it's not because I told her. Monica and Donlynne got to trading insults and I had to cut the meeting short."

Monica was one of those sistahs who reminded you of Erykah Badu or one of those other alternative sistahs, conscious, natural hair and scarf wearing, African or Caribbean garb wearing sistahs. No makeup, gold or silver jewelry or other superficial enhancements. She could sing like Sarah Vaughn and she had an old spirit about her. She was a well-known vegetarian and very supportive of art and holistic organizations. I remember last year she made a big deal to campaign that the cafeteria be more considerate of those who did not include meat in their diet and to practice Kosher or Halal cooking for the black Jews and Muslim population on campus.

Monica was also a cofounder of the Anti-Greek Federation or AGF as they are more commonly known. Each year, the Black Greek Letter Organizations coming out shows would be interesting because the AGF was always up to something. If they weren't bringing posters stating their position, they were doing things to disrupt the organizations' programs. Personally, I didn't see how she was going to run and gain support of the majority on campus. The fraternity and sorority members on the yard may have been small in number, but they were very influential. Plus, that kind of personality wouldn't gather a lot of support because no one would want to be associated with an organization that was viewed as negative. Monica and I have never bumped heads personally, but I already knew how she felt about me. She once made a big deal about the fact that I had been intimate with Aaliyah and another member of their sorority. Forget the fact that I wasn't messing with the women at the same time or that they weren't in the sorority at the time. But our less than six degrees of separation was enough for her to make much ado about nothing. That was one of the worst things about attending an HBCU, sometimes, people wouldn't let go of the high school games and felt the need to put everyone on Front Street.

Here we were at the end of October and we knew that Donlynne, Monica, Mary and Elicia were running for Miss NC Tech. Not a bad competition and it would be fair to say an interesting one.

"So how do you feel about Monica running?" I asked.

"You know, I don't have an opinion about her running. I'm not going to let her stop me. I know that it would be fair to say that she will be able to attack Donlynne and I directly because of our membership in our sororities, but she would have her hands full if she confronted Mary. I love sister girl, but you and I both know that Mary is a fashion diva and their personalities clash. In fact, Mary is the epitome of everything Monica hates."

That was true. I liked how Elicia was playing her cards. She was keeping her mouth shut, which was good for us. Sometimes, publicity can work against you. If everyone knows what you are doing, then there is no element of surprise. I'm not supporting being sneaky, but there is a time to talk and a time to walk. I hated to see Donlynne play her cards like that because she can be a nice, lovable girl. At the same time, she's going for the jugular every time she gets into it with someone.

"Officially, Elite has never endorsed a candidate for Miss NC Tech. There are usually at least two members who consider running so each woman would have to fend for herself. Plus, there's the conflict of interest because each new Miss NC Tech would be invited and usually accepts membership in the organization."

"Wow, that sucks."

"Why you say that?"

"I was hoping that you could use your influence as president to secure an endorsement from the group."

"I still have influence, but the ladies are going to endorse who they want to endorse. Sometimes, it's a catty thing of they'll endorse you if you endorse them and I don't want to get caught up in that. Especially if the other candidates change their platforms or align themselves with candidates I don't want to be associated with."

That's true, "I just thought of something. What did Arnisha think?"

"Sometimes when you can't say a word all you do is hum a melody. But I'm sure that she will address that at the interest meeting on Sunday."

"This Sunday?"

"Yes, this Sunday. Time is flying fast ain't it?"

"It is."

Once we had arrived at Elicia's dorm, I watched as she went up the building to make sure she got in okay. Then I went back to my suite so I could study for my other classes.

Thank You, Lord

The NC Tech Idol competition was coming off well. The idea was that each act had three minutes to sing a song. Then the audience had thirty minutes to vote on the acts they wanted to stay. The two acts with the least amount of votes were eliminated after each round. Each act paid two dollars to participate in the selection process and then another dollar if they qualified. Then each vote costs a quarter and the votes were pre-sold. We raised $3500 total and students were allowed to participate as volunteers for their community service credits. Personally, I was feeling the idea because the money was already raised and if people wanted to donate more they could, plus the Sickle Cell Anemia Association would know in advance what they were looking to collect, which was a good look for us, too.

There were seven acts that qualified to be in the show: three groups and four solo acts. Mostly, we had R&B and rap performances. I think one of the acts said they would be doing gospel as well. Elicia and I were selected to be part of a group that sold tickets for the event.

"For the first act, we have *The Greensboro Four* singing 'Can You Stand the Rain.'"

These four young men were paying homage to the four young men who refused to give up their seats at the counter at Woolworth that helped ignite the sit-in movements. Their a cappella was a nice way to start the performance. As other groups got to go through their performances, people started buying more tickets.

"For a minute there, I think you forgot about me," Elicia said while we were selling tickets. Faith went back to Raleigh to go to church with some friends. Today was the first time in a week Elicia and I were able to hang out and get the program going. She had been busy with her school work, planning her campaign and helping Arnie with his monthly presentations until we kept missing each other. Not to be outdone, I've actually been in a serious relationship with Faith and spending a lot of time with her.

"I'm always here," I gave her a hug.

"So how is she? I know you are excited," I opened the door and let her in the booth. Mary was preparing for her surprise performance at the event so it was just going to be the two of us for a while.

"She's good," I replied as I opened the register to give another student their set of tickets. "I didn't think I would fall in love as fast as I have but I'm glad I'm in love with her."

"That's good. I'm just working and going to school. I've built up a nice client base at M.Walker so I have that to look forward to as well as working at Miriam and Mary. Mary got me going to Tokyo next week for some kind of show. I forgot the name of it."

"Tokyo? The semester is almost over with." I wasn't hating, but I was concerned with the trip being close to finals week and this was the time that professors piled on more work and the generous ones sponsored extra study sessions. I didn't want to see Elicia's GPA slip and she become ineligible to run in the election.

"We're meeting with some people who want to sell the line in Tokyo. We'll be staying near an Army base there. Actually, it's a black Japanese couple that is interested in the project."

"That's what I'm talking about. Mary Braxton is doing some big things."

"She is. If you were to come to our suite right now, you would see mine and Mary's bags packed at the door. As nervous as we are, we're ready to go," she stopped so she could sell two more tickets. "We had to arrange to take two of our finals early."

I used to want to shoot a video in China. Back in the year 2000 when wearing Chinese letters was popular and everyone was wearing them that seemed to be the thing to do. Once I researched the idea, I had dropped the idea. We couldn't have pulled off the idea if I had wanted to and I couldn't afford to lose any money. But fashion was a lot different. You could do a lot with fashion and all you needed was the right people, with the right ideas, with the right mindset and you were good to go.

"So are you going to go to church in Tokyo?" I asked.

"That is what I'm looking forward to. I hear there is a small church near the army base we'll be staying at plus, I want to get a copy of the Bible written in Japanese as a keepsake. Just to see how they do it. I'm thinking this is going to be fun."

"Yeah, Japan has always been open to Western ideas and concepts."

Once the show got down to the two final contestants, the volunteers were rotating shifts and we were moved into a room where we were counting ballots. They put the show on the television screen so we could see Mary's halftime show. Mary was wearing a black, white and red kimono with chopsticks in her hair and a shoe called a Zori that had a V-shaped thong that came across the big toe and the rest of the foot.

"Her earrings say 'life,'" Elicia was telling me. I moved closer to the screen but the letters were so small I couldn't see it.

Once the show was over, we went back to counting the ballots. I also understood why the volunteers needed a break. There were a bunch of tickets that needed to be counted and I didn't want to imagine how many tickets were sold.

"Can you see yourself marrying Faith?" Elicia asked me while we were counting.

"I don't know. I haven't thought that far ahead yet."

"When my mother and father were getting married, my mom said that dad knew within six weeks he wanted to marry my mom."

I remember that she had told me that once before when we were younger. I had just shrugged it off then but I could see where she was going with it. A lot of people who went to college in Greensboro ended up marrying the person they were dating in school. "I'm just going to follow the flow and let Him lead me in that direction. He hasn't revealed that to me yet. That's not to say that He won't lead me in that direction."

"I feel you," Elicia continued to count. "I stay so busy until I don't feel like I have time for a man."

"Your man will find you, don't worry. It will happen in His time."

"I'm glad you feel that way. But I don't worry about it too much. I'm keeping busy with the makeup and the clothes and of course, building my relationship with Him."

"You got to stay busy with that. So many different ideas are presented on this campus that you always have to have that discernment about which ideas are good and which ones aren't."

It took another hour for Elicia, I and the rest of the volunteers to finish counting the ballots. I couldn't wait to see who had won the contest. We got to join the audience in the auditorium once all the counting was done. When we were seated, Arnisha and Malachai were presenting the Sickle Cell Anemia Association a check for seventy five hundred dollars. Not bad for a group of college students who always claimed to be broke. We are financially challenged because we spent our money on books, supplies, tuition and room and board or an apartment and the expenses that came with keeping up with that.

Once the winner was announced and the crowd had cleared, the whole executive board along with a few attendants and helpers took a trip to Applebee's. It had been a while since I had been to Applebee's. The last time I was there was when members of the crew and I had finished a shoot near the Four Seasons Mall.

When we got seated, Aaliyah was acting a fool as usual, hating and trying to threaten Donlynne. Everyone else ignored the drama between the two and Donlynne for her part seemed more interested in what Arnie was doing or saying. Once we finished eating our food and paying our tips, we made the trip to Elicia and Mary's suite. We ended up watching *Woman Thou Art Loosed* on BET and debated the drama that the character went through. It was almost like men versus women because Elicia, Arnisha, Donlynne, Aaliyah and Gabrielle took the woman's side and Malachai, Arnie, Amir, Ezekiel and I took the guy's side. Then we watched some of the Madea plays and were trying to find the scriptures he was referencing in the Bible. We were having so much fun that I didn't realize it was 4:30 in the morning when I left the suite.

"So, we are going to meet at the library tomorrow before Mary and I go to the airport right?"

"Yeah," I said, "I'm calling Faith tomorrow to let her know that I'm seeing you off."

"Good, good. I want to make sure that I get to spend enough time with you before I go to Japan. You know Mary and I have to represent NC Tech while we're there. It's funny, I used to get mad when we had to do all those presentations in class. Now, I'm glad we had all those presentations to prepare us for where we have to go. You know that winning a contract or striking a deal is not always about how good you look, but about the best presentation. The one who puts on the best presentation is the one who will win the contract. And I want our presentation to be the best."

"And it will be," Aaliyah commented as we were getting ready to leave. We all got up to give Elicia a hug so she could get some rest before she got on that plane and headed out to Japan. She was looking at a twenty one hour flight and she was going to need all the rest she could get. I walked to the door and Aaliyah closed it behind me. She was a character. I'll be happy when she can find a man to manage her handful and boy does Aaliyah have an attitude on her. She was a perfectionist and she wants everything to be just right, and if it's not done *exactly* to her specifications, then she wants it done again. But that's Aaliyah for you. Aaliyah's not a bad person. Her parents are NC Tech alumni and they give a substantial amount of money to the school each year. Being the only girl in the family with three boys, it was easy to see why she was spoiled.

"Alright," I responded and I gave her a hug. The hug lingered longer than I thought it should have I let that thought pass. I checked my pockets to see if I had my keys, my ID card and my wallet. I didn't want to have to come back at almost five in the morning for anything else. I walked back to my suite and I was surprised to see NC Tech police were carrying someone out in handcuffs. I would've stayed and watched to be nosey, but I was also sleepy and I wanted to take a bath before I hit the sheets. I looked to the sky and gave a quick prayer for the student being led out and thanked Him that this was not being done in broad daylight. When I got to the door of the dorm, I seen a few guys creeping back to the dorms they live in, or leaving with girls they were going to take home. Hmm…this was what I miss every day at this time of night, I should make an appointment to stay up more often. I took out my cell phone and called Elicia to let her know I got to my room okay. I listened to the phone ring five times and when the answering machine came on I clicked the phone off and put it back in my pocket. She'll be alright.

Order My Steps

*A*rnisha was wearing a dark blue business suit resembling the dark blue suits other members of the SGA officers wore. Some of the cafeteria workers were setting up refreshments for potential candidates and their guests who were getting ready to come into the ballroom. Malachai and other SGA officers were sitting off to the side, watching everyone as they came in.

Donlynne and her campaign team were in there deep. They all were wearing her sorority's colors and had taken up the first two rows. She wore a navy blue business suit and shades. She took her seat amongst members of the executive board. I smiled on the inside, only to keep myself from laughing at her. Monica and the members of AGF were also in attendance. They all were wearing shirts that said:

no letters, all betters

"Let me find out that I should have brought my team," Elicia nudged me on my shoulder.

"I should have brought mine, too," Mary agreed. She had walked in with Arnez. I was happy to see the man was feeling better and walking about. He still had a few bandages and his shoulder was in a sling, but other than that, he was good. Mary and Elicia hugged and they took their seats together.

"I saw you on the tape Donte, you represented for me," Arnez gave me a pound and my first compliment about being on video but not *the* videos.

"No doubt."

We watched as more and more students were coming in and taking their seats. Arnisha had saw me and smiled. When it was 7:00 p.m., Arnisha called for everyone's attention.

"First, I want to give God all the glory that we were able to meet today. I want to open the meeting with a prayer," Arnisha began and almost every head was bowed.

"I don't mean to interrupt," Monica barked as she stood up, "do we have to open the meeting with prayer? I don't want to offend anyone who isn't a Christian."

If eyes could shoot daggers Monica would be dead. Arnisha started to scold her but I could tell she was holding her tongue. "Make me aware of that the next time *you* put together this presentation."

A few chuckles were heard from the executive board and Arnisha read Psalm 131.

"O LORD, my heart is not lifted up, my eyes are not raised too high; I do not occupy myself with things too great and too marvelous for me. But I have calmed and quieted my soul, like a weaned child with its mother; my soul is like the weaned child that is with me. O Israel, hope in the LORD from this time on and forever more."

"Solomon teaches us in Proverbs 31:25 that the clothing of a virtuous woman is not in the crown of my head or the gown that I wear, but in strength and honor. He also says that favor is deceitful and beauty is vain; but a woman that feareth the Lord shall be praised.

"This is what I think of when I reflect on the women whom I have had the privilege of sharing the title Miss NC Tech. It wasn't about what America or North Carolina Technical University said was beautiful. It was about the value of a woman's character that made her beautiful.

"Ladies, we wake up in the morning and put on this makeup; make sure our hair is done right and put on some nice smelling lotions and perfumes. But how many of us wake up with a prayer on our hearts? How many of us think about ways we can help better our community, or worry if the time we spend tutoring the children is helping them understand the material? We check to make sure our pedicure is tight before we check to see if our hearts are right.

"I don't know how many of you plan to seek the title, but I do know that whoever wins will have to be willing to put in twice as much work as I have. On the outside, you may think all I do is stand around and look pretty, but on the inside, I realize that there is a lot of work to do. I am expected to be at major events and functions in Greensboro and across North Carolina representing our school. I'm expected to fill in at a moment's notice to be a presenter, a speaker or an escort. I also have to plan coronation, the Miss NC Tech luncheon for all past Miss NC Techs, organize the school's service project, *this* interest meeting as well as sit in on SGA meetings and on different organization committees throughout campus.

"All of this and I have to not only come in with a 3.0; I have to maintain it. I have to make time for myself, enjoy being on campus and hanging out with my friends as well as purse goals and aspirations that interest me. Not to mention that my stipend barely keeps my hair done, nails nice, makeup right, clothes clean and the physical appearance that I am expected to uphold before I can enjoy life.

"And this is not a complaint. This is part of the written and unwritten job description. It is what makes me and every Miss NC Tech a virtuous woman."

The room was in applause and in agreement that Arnisha fits the bill. Elicia was pointing to her eyes to point out that Arnisha was wearing the same shade she was. Only a woman would notice that, or that was how well she knew her customer.

"I've talked to several of you in private," Arnisha continued, "but reaching your goal to be Miss NC Tech will ultimately be on you. I'm going to give you guys a few pointers before I take questions. This campaign is going to be very expensive. I'm not going to suggest a number, only to say that in some cases, it can be worth more than a semester of in-state tuition."

"Darn," I thought heard someone yell in the crowd- maybe they said something else. A few laughs were heard but soon the room got quiet again.

"I know some of you got your teams together, and that is fine because you need to prepare to run this race. But you need to be cautious of your actions because any unauthorized gathering or announcement can cause you to be disqualified. I have seen firsthand one too many women lose the opportunity because she was not discreet. So please be careful. If there are any questions—"

Before Arnisha could finish her sentence, Monica had walked to the microphone. She took command of the mic and held it as if she was going to belt one of her infamous numbers. Truthfully, that would be the only thing the majority of us would have been interested in hearing from her.

"I just want to know…how much is involved in this campaign? You said more than a semester of in-state tuition…that's at least a G right? What dollar amount do you think we are looking at?"

"Well, in the last two elections, the average campaign cost each candidate about $3500…"

"$3500?" Monica interrupted.

"Well let's see, I had a pizza party for my team when I officially announced that I was running. I spent a lot of time on the road meeting with local business leaders as well as traveling back to Charlotte to gain support and funds. I had new suits I needed to buy and I had a photo shoot and my website that I still pay for to update students on coming events. Don't forget that the fliers, the posters, the banners and getting Trin-I-Tee to perform the day of the election. Even though the ladies were nice enough not to charge me their full asking price and they did this as a *huge favor* to my father, getting them was not cheap and fortunately I had a co-sponsor with that.

"But for real, a lot of candidates had sponsors and prepared what they were going to spend their money on well in advance. The purpose is not to spend a lot of money on your campaign. The purpose is to plan an effective campaign and to utilize all the resources at your disposal."

Donlynne walked to the microphone, "When are the applications going to be distributed?"

"Applications will be given out February 7 and will be due February 21."

This French vanilla beauty walked to the mic. Her hair was in a free form afro like Jill Scott. The natural shades of her makeup seamed to bring out her eyes. As the brothers would say, she had a bit of meat on her bones, but she was not overweight.

"What are the limits on how much we can campaign?"

That's when her name came to me. Daisy Roxboro. She wasn't really a known woman around campus. I've seen her at a function here and there, but that was about it. Donlynne cut her eyes at her while Daisy was waiting on her question to be answered.

"Well, when you pick up your applications, a set of guidelines will be given out about the campaign. But I'm going to be honest with you; this campaign is going to bring out the best in you, and others will take this opportunity to bring out the worst in you. The worst way to start out your reign as Miss North Carolina Technical University is to have a lot of enemies. These very women that you run against, you will need them at one point or another to help you get your agenda across. Your opponent may be the head of an organization that can get your project off the ground. Or she may be part of the sorority that does a program that you can seek advice from or possibly work with. I'm not going to say that all of you are going to be friends. But do unto others as if you were the others."

I saw Elicia and Mary look at one another. A part of me wondered if their friendship would last at the end of the election.

Give Me a Clean Heart

aith went with me to the airport to see Elicia and Mary off to Japan. I'm really happy for those two because they have worked extremely hard to get to where they are, and I knew that God was going to continue to bless them. Even if the potential partnership doesn't work out, I'm sure that He knows which doors to open and which ones to leave closed.

The drive from NC Tech to Piedmont Triad International Airport was about twenty minutes; partly because most people who get on I-40 think it's a NASCAR race track. To keep up with traffic, I was speeding doing about eighty miles per hour. This was all good until I saw a sea of cars come to a halt. If it weren't for the new brakes I had installed a month ago, we would have crashed into the car in front of us. The car behind us almost hit us and had to skid to the side of the road just to avoid us. Two miles away from the airport exit, they were still working on the interstate. After a while, Faith and I arrived at her room. I was helping her pack to go home for Thanksgiving break. To Faith's credit, she already had a large portion of the packing done—she just needed some help in her room and putting the boxes in the car. I had agreed to give Faith a ride to the bus stop and to ship the boxes for her.

We stepped into her bedroom to help her fold clothes that she was taking home. She had two piles of clothes, the first pile was for clothes that she was bring back and the next pile was for clothes that she wasn't bringing back. She had boxes for things she was shipping home that she wasn't bringing back either.

"I can't believe I have so much stuff here," Faith said.

"Probably not as much as I got."

"But that's different, you can drive back and forth to Winston anytime you want to. I have to bring as much stuff from Raleigh as possible because I can't just up and go home when I please. Besides, you know I don't have a car."

That was true, Faith mainly took the bus around town when she wanted to go somewhere if she could not get a ride from a friend. Faith told me earlier that the car she had two years ago crashed and she hasn't tried to get a car since. Some of our dates have consisted of us going to the dealerships on Wendover and looking for cars, but she hasn't found one she was looking for. I had yet to find one to replace the Continental so I was making it work for the moment.

I sat down on the bed and eventually laid down on my back. I was a little tired from all of the packing and moving around I was doing. I still had to go to my place and pack up my things so I could go back to Winston-Salem tomorrow. I'm not complaining though. Faith sat down next to me and then looked back.

"So are we going to try to meet sometime after Christmas?"

I knew the answer was no. My family was talking about going to Raleigh to spend some time with some relatives and even if we didn't go, I knew that I wouldn't get two minutes alone to spend with anyone, especially a woman I hadn't brought home to meet my parents yet. "What are you doing New Years?"

"I'll probably be at my church. They are having Watch Night to celebrate the New Year. I've never been to a Watch Night service before."

"What is a Watch Night service?"

"My friend told me that what they did last year was testify about how good the Lord has been to them the previous year. The pastor spoke and gave some encouraging words and then they watched the clock turn twelve. They had a special communion and sang hymns and praises. Some people stayed at the church until the next morning and they serve a big breakfast for the New Year."

I sat up. "That sounds like something I would be interested in. I say, count me in."

Our faces leaned closer together and we shared a kiss. Faith got up and she went to packing some more things and I took some of the bags to my car. We had never kissed before and not that it was an awkward kiss. It was a pretty good one...almost innocent-like. I finished loading the car she was renting with things she was taking to Raleigh and we set aside a spot in the suite for all the things she was mailing. I went back to her room and sat on her bed and turned on the television. I turned to the TCT channel but I didn't see anyone I wanted to look at so I flipped the channels to see who was on.

"We can always pop in a movie," Faith suggested.

"A movie is good."

She put on *Love and Basketball* and the movie took me back to my prom night. I felt guilty because Elicia and I had just broken up and I had broken her heart when she found out that I had decided to make movies. She chose to go solo while I would film my first video on prom night. I had set it up so I wouldn't have to think about her or that night. I met up with this older woman I hooked up with on the internet and we went to see *Love and Basketball.* After we saw the movie, we went to her place and she showed me how she was making money making videos and I was hooked. I think we did a part one and a part two. After that, I swore off the movie because it always brought the memories of my first movie to mind.

"Is something wrong?" Faith asked.

"If I could take back my senior prom, I would have found a better use of my time."

"What happened?"

"After I saw this movie, I made my first video. And it's not that I blame the movie...I liked the movie when I saw it but the first video always comes to mind when I think of this movie."

Faith turned the movie off and we start watching *Inkwell* instead. Faith got up and brought back a slice of cheesecake she was able to get from The Living Room Book and Pastry the night before. *Inkwell* had a lot of positive memories for me and I could relate to the main character in how I saw my life. In fact, parts of it were identical. Needless to say, I loved this movie. Elicia and I used to watch it all the time. A part of me wanted to run to the airport and try to get a ticket to Tokyo and surprise them, but I couldn't leave Faith and I wouldn't have anywhere to stay.

Faith and I were feeding each other cheesecake and somewhere in the middle of feeding cheesecake and flirting, we were sharing another kiss. We caught each other again and sat up on the bed.

"We should probably leave the bedroom," Faith said, "Don't want you to get any ideas."

"Actually, that's a real good idea."

We got up and we started watching *Inkwell* in the living room. As she leaned next to me I kissed her. I don't know why I did, but I felt like kissing her. She didn't object and next thing you know she was laying on me and we were kissing. I was feeling tempted to take it to another level.

"We should stop."

"Yeah, I think it's best if I go."

"Yeah, that might be a good idea. I don't want us to do something we might regret."

"Me either."

I got up and pulled my keys out so I could go. I turned around and I meant to give Faith a kiss on the cheeks but I kissed her on the mouth instead. We kissed against the wall and my shirt came off and after a while her shirt was coming off, too. After I got to the ground, I was trying to find the will to get up but my flesh wanted this. It has been over a year since I had been intimate with anyone. I had one minor relapse after I got saved but that was one time and I had promised God I wasn't going to do it again. As my pants were coming down, I started to ask the Lord for forgiveness because I didn't think I was going to be able to stop. Faith sat up and I sat up next to her.

"I haven't done this in a few years," she confided in me. She reached over and played with my chest.

"I haven't either. And I said I wasn't going to either."

"Are we going to stop?"

I had the perfect opportunity to get up and put my pants on. I thought about God and disappointing the Spirit. And then I thought I had already taken things far enough. We kissed one more time and I couldn't tell where this kiss was going to lead. Either I was going to obey the Lord and leave or I was going to go forward with this with the hope I could repent for it later.

*****

I was going to do it. It had been almost a year since I had been with a woman and I was going to do it. But just when I looked down at her, getting ready to fornicate, I couldn't hold it up. It was embarrassing because it had never happened to me before. I'll admit, I was going to try again and then I felt her arm wrap around my shoulder. That's when my conviction set in.

"Maybe it's best if we don't do it," Faith moved from under me and put her shirt on.

"Yeah, we should wait."

I'll admit, I've had more feelings for Faith then I have had for any other woman I had been with. But this didn't feel right. It's almost like I had an obligation not to ruin her for her wedding night, be it with me or someone else. Now had I been on the job, I surely would have been embarrassed. As I put on the rest of my clothes, I got up and helped her up. For the first time I was speechless. I gave her a hug and I took her things to the car so I could take her to the bus station.

Ain't-a That Good News

$\mathcal{M}$essing around with Madea this morning almost made me late for church. I try to watch part of a Tyler Perry movie each Sunday before I got to church. For me, the movies are like therapy and a Sunday School lesson rolled into one. I liked Tyler's plays and even more importantly, I appreciated his commentary. As I have spent time learning how to accept myself, I found that I'm not the only one in my condition.

Ezekiel was knocking on the door and trying to come in. Most Sunday mornings, I left the door unlocked so that he could just come in. I was tying my tie around my neck and trying to unlock the door. He walked in and was shaking his head.

"Man, you supposed to have been ready by now."

"You know I've been studying for my classes and trying to make sure Elicia's campaign is tight. I've been on the phone with vendors and trying to bargain some prices within our budget."

"I hear you on that. February hasn't even come in and you guys are on a ball."

"I got to be. We're doing a lot of this work over the Christmas holiday."

"I feel you."

After everything was in place, I grabbed my Bible and highlighter and walked out of the door. Ezekiel was driving his 1987 Honda Accord. I used to pick on him about the dents and the scratches and him not having any rims. I quit when he came back with how much he was saving in gas and how the car was as priceless as a man's soul because it got him from Point A to Point B and was well maintained. My spirit had some dents and scratches in it too, so I didn't gain by pointing his out.

We got to the church and saw that Elicia, Aaliyah and Mary were standing outside talking. We honked to make our presence known. Several of the members and the visitors were arriving. Rahliem was the guest speaker and this was exciting. I'd always heard about the man talking about his ministry but this would be the first time I'd ever heard him preach the Word. I didn't even know he was coming until Ezekiel said something about it when he called to wake me up.

We had barely gotten to our seats in the church when we saw Mary was singing in the choir that was walking in authority, casting out the demons and praising our Lord at the same time. I was so into the performance, I grabbed a piece of paper and waved it in the air. Thinking of Donnie McClurkin's song, I wondered what he would have said if he were to walk in.

The church announcements were read and the choir performed another selection. Time seemed to have gone fast because I was anticipating Rahliem's interpretation of the Word. When we got the tithes and offerings, I remembered that I left the church's money in the room. Ezekiel rushing me made me forget. I wrote a small note on my program to put aside the money for next week's collection. We prayed for those whose concerns were brought before the church. After the choir sang again, Rahliem got up to speak.

"Everyone pull out your swords and let's go to Matthew 15:10-20. For those of you who are starting your journey with us today, I always encourage you to BYOB, bring your own Bibles. So that when I read the verses my brothers and sisters can follow along and make sure that I am reading what you are reading. Don't want me to change a word or two and get out of the Book, or make up some stuff as I go along."

There was small laughter in the room. The flickering of the pages made Rahliem and the Reverend smile.

"And he called the multitude, and said unto them, Hear, and understand: Not that which goeth into the mouth defileth a man; but that which cometh out of the mouth, this defileth a man. Then came his disciples, and said unto him, Knowest thou that the Pharisees were offended, after they heard this saying? But he answered and said, Every plant, which my heavenly Father hath not planted, shall be rooted up. Let them alone: they be blind leaders of the blind. And if the blind lead the blind, both shall fall into the ditch. Then answered Peter and said unto him, Declare unto us this parable. And Jesus said, Are ye also yet without understanding? Do not ye yet understand, that whatsoever entereth in at the mouth goeth into the belly, and is cast out into the draught? But those things which proceed out of the mouth come forth from the heart; and they defile the man. For out of the heart proceed evil thoughts, murders, adulteries, fornications, thefts, false witness, blasphemies: These are the things which defile a man: but to eat with unwashen hands defileth not a man.

"Now for those of you who have the New Revised Standard Version, your text will read like this:

Then he called the crowd to him and said to them, "Listen and understand: it is not what goes into the mouth that defiles a person, but it is what comes out of the mouth that defiles." Then the disciples approached and said to him, "Do you know that the Pharisees took offense when they heard what you said?" He answered, "Every plant that my heavenly Father has not planted will be uprooted. Let them alone; they are blind guides of the blind. And if one blind person guides another, both will fall into a pit." But Peter said to him, "Explain this parable to us." Then he said, "Are you also still without understanding? Do you not see that whatever goes into the mouth enters the stomach, and goes out into the sewer? But what comes out of the mouth proceeds from the heart, and this is what defiles. For out of the heart come evil intentions, murder, adultery, fornication, theft, false witness, slander. These are what defile a person, but to eat with unwashed hands does not defile.

"Your tongue is a mighty weapon brothers and sisters and it can be used for good and evil. Paul warns us in the book of Romans 14:13-23 when he says *Let us therefore no longer pass judgment on one another, but resolve instead never to put a stumbling block or hindrance in the way of another. I know and am persuaded in the Lord Jesus that nothing is unclean in itself; but it is unclean for anyone who thinks it unclean. If your brother or sister is being injured by what you eat, you are no longer walking in love. Do not let what you eat cause the ruin of one for whom Christ died. So do not let your good be spoken of as evil. For the kingdom of God is not food and drink but righteousness and peace and joy in the Holy Spirit. The one who thus serves Christ is acceptable to God and has human approval. Let us then pursue what makes for peace and for mutual up building. Do not, for the sake of food, destroy the work of God. Everything is indeed clean, but it is wrong for you to make others fall by what you eat; it is good not to eat meat or drink wine or do anything that makes your brother or sister stumble. The faith that you have, have as your own conviction before God. Blessed are those who have no reason to condemn themselves because of what they approve. But those who have doubts are condemned if they eat, because they do not act from faith; for whatever does not proceed from faith is sin.*

"Now that we have read the two different texts concerning the tongue, would you agree my brothers and sisters it is about time that we watch what we say?"

Rahliem looked up and saw that the church was in agreement. He continued, "When slavery existed in this country, the slave masters used to refer to our ancestors as niggers, or they compared our people to animals. When they described our features, we were, *strong* as an ox; he had *horse's teeth.* They would "breed" us to get desirable traits. And how do you think those names and characteristics made our people feel?"

"Angry," one person shouted in the congregation.

"Hurt," another one said.

"Like we're not even human," I could hear Mary say.

"I'm going to use that one sister, if you don't mind," Rahliem waited for an approval before he continued, "being compared to an animal does make you feel like you're not even human. When you are being degraded, you lose your confidence and self-worth. We listen to our music today and isn't that what you hear? These superstars on the videos and our brothers on the streets calling our sisters B's and H's."

Slight scoffs filled the room as it was not left to the imagination what he was referring to.

"And what's worse, hearing our sisters calling others and *themselves* that. I was at the gas station on Martin Luther King, Jr. Drive this morning and I saw two young ladies walking by:

"What's up B?

"Hey H how you doing?

"With a hug and embrace. Now see, if I would've walked up to that same girl and been like *hey B...*"

The women in the church turned to one another and I could hear them get excited, "No he didn't!"

"I wish he *would* walk up to me with that mess...I'd hey B him."

"Brothers we're no better, we call each other niggers and MF"ers all day long."

The church got excited once again, like they had never heard the word before. Well, maybe they haven't heard the words referenced in a sermon before.

"Y'all know what I'm talking about, I'm telling the truth. Women call us some trifling niggers. I see some of y'all guilty of that. Now when we read 1 John 3:2 we are called Children of God. We're given that title in 1 John 5:19 and in Philippians 2:15 and in John 1:12 just to name a few. Another text, Romans 8:17, we are referred to as co-heirs with Christ. Throughout Paul's numerous letters to the Church he calls us brethren, including the women too. Now you know when Jesus comes, we're not going to be able to walk up to him and say 'what's up my Nigga!'"

A bunch of negative affirmations and laughter filled the room. I think if the Pastor had been white, she would have blushed.

"Now y'all have to forgive me, as I'm used to winning souls in the streets, but my point is this. We need to be more careful with how we refer to each other, my brothers and sisters, my neighbors, my joint-heirs with Christ. And while we're calling them that, who do you think is listening?"

"Jesus," some of the elders said and nodded their heads sharply.

"The children," I heard some of the women say. I wonder if some of them had covered their children's ears during parts of Rahliem's sermon.

"The children listen to what we call ourselves and how we address one another. Mama got something bad to say about the daddy and soon, the child believes that about her daddy. Why? Because he or she heard their mama say it over and over again.

"And while these children believe what they hear, let's talk about the names that we call them. Little minds are not even developed yet and we automatically calling them names.

"Lazy, stupid, slow, ignorant, troubled…these and many more names are what we call our children. If you seen the show *Sanford and Son*, the son, Lamont Sanford made a quote about how he thought his name was Dummy Sanford until he was twenty years old. Why? Because his father called him that over and over and over again. What his father was doing, and what we are doing is sowing seeds. Now when we sow our seeds, the Lord says they're supposed to bear fruit. But when you call a child ugly, you are planting those seeds of low self-esteem, self-hatred and suicide into that very fertile soil that is the child's mind.

That child looks in the mirror and they don't love themselves. Why? Because they believe and hang on to every word you say. Can you point out anywhere in the Bible where God belittled His creation? Even when He was upset or disappointed in His creation, did He ever acknowledge us other than by our names?

"We walk around with those 'What Would Jesus Do?' paraphernalia on and I'm telling you, Jesus wouldn't be calling us names. So why do you call your children that? Why address your wife in that manner? Why call yourself that? Husbands, did you know that every time you belittle or deprive your wives, you are doing that to yourselves because you are supposed to be one?

"Jesus has commanded that we love God with all our hearts, all our minds and all our soul. And the second commandment is that we love our neighbors as we love ourselves. We can't show people love if we are calling them out of their names. Would you say these things to God if He were standing right here? Most of you would say no and I would say that you shouldn't say those names to others."

Rahliem took his seat next to the Pastor. I was looking forward to the day when he would have his own congregation. I never saw it like that and I didn't know that people believed they were the names they were called. I could see the little children grabbing onto names like "dummy" and "lazy" and claiming the names as their own.

When the Pastor called for people to accept Jesus as their personal Lord and Savior, this young man who probably went to school with us, got up and started walking to the front. The walk looked slow and the Pastor was encouraging him to move forward. I remembered when I had made that journey. I felt that I had these people and demons tugging me at the sides trying to prevent me from making the journey. I felt a hand pushing me forward and I thought that someone was guiding my path to the altar. As I got closer, I felt the people and the demons falling away. When the young man reached and touched the Pastor's hand, I smiled a sigh of relief. He had begun the journey, just as I knew he would.

***

As service came to an end, I met up with Rahliem, Abednego, and Celtius. I was slightly disappointed to see that Mya was not in attendance. I knew that Neal was at the dorm studying for his final that he had the next morning.

"That was a very good sermon," I heard Ezekiel compliment Rahliem. Rahliem reached for his black Kangol hat that was hanging on the coat rack outside of the sanctuary. All of the members of the congregation and the visiting members of the church had shaken his hand and the pastor's hand early on.

"I never thought about names like that until you said something," Abednego jumped in, "I felt convicted because my brothers and I call each other names all the time."

"Well, I'm glad that Jesus allowed me to be used so I could give you a message that aligns with his spirit."

I was quiet as I thought about the sin Faith and I almost committed. I wondered what name she was calling me.

"I had wanted to speak about temptation and how it is difficult to keep the flesh from going against the will of the Spirit and that was what I'd told the pastor I would be speaking on." Rahliem revealed as we followed him across the street to one of the houses next to the dorms at A&T. Rahliem reached in his hand and he pulled out a key and unlocked the door, letting us in. I was surprised that he knew someone who lived in the area that would entrust him with the house. Inside, I could see the vintage themed furniture and styling that came from the seventies. "But when I woke up, He had a different plan and I followed."

Rahliem picked up some papers that were on the end table.

"Who hooked you up with this place?" Abednego asked as he sat on the sofa that crunched due to the plastic wrapping that was still on it.

"This is a rental property that is owned by Jalail Stevens, one of the vice presidents of M. Walker. He knew I was coming to speak and offered me to use the space, even though Winston wasn't that far away."

"That's what's up." Abednego picked up the remote and turned on the television. We followed Rahliem into the kitchen where buckets of fried chicken were placed on the counter along with macaroni and cheese, mashed potatoes, green beans and buttermilk biscuits. Everyone grabbed a plate and filled it to their hearts' content and they fixed cups of sweet tea that were in the refrigerator.

"I see he sent someone to hook us up while I was giving my sermon." Rahliem sat down after he took a sip of his drink. He led us in blessing the food and then we sat down around the table and got into our meals. "I was gonna just order some pizza, but I do appreciate this food."

"Yeah…" Ezekiel struggled to chew his food. "This is good. I'm gonna have to keep this company in mind next time I want something catered."

I looked at the boxes and noticed Mountain Fried Chicken's name on the package. I filed that note into my memory bank.

"How are y'all gonna eat and not invite a brother to get a plate?" Abednego complained as he stood in the entryway of the television and watched all of us sit down to eat and fellowship.

"You should've followed us in here and you would've had a plate, too." Celtius responded.

"Yeah," Rahliem jumped in. "I don't tell grown men when to eat. Go ahead and fix you a plate."

Abednego walked to the counter and grabbed a plate and fixed his own food. "How do you face temptation?" He threw the question out there and everyone's head lifted from the table. "I would've loved to hear your sermon on that because I can't leave the gin and juice alone."

"What you mean you can't leave it alone?" Ezekiel was puzzled as he put his drink down. "You throw the bottles of gin out and you drive past the ABC Store when you see it."

"Addictions are not that easy to battle Ezekiel," Rahliem said after he had finished chewing his food. "We all have our vices—our shortcomings that we struggle with matter how much we pray them away. I've been smoking weed and gambling since I was thirteen. I don't tell y'all that for you to repeat it, but to point out a thorn in my side that I need to work on. I can identify with Abednego's need to drink because sometimes, when I get real angry, to keep from getting violent and spazzing out on someone, I'll get me a joint just so I can relax and calm my nerves."

"I like to fight," Celtius admitted. "Nothing pumps my nerves than stepping one on one with a dude and knocking his lights out."

"I'm not saying everyone admit their vices because I'm sure some of us don't want to share," Rahliem spoke up. I saw the way Ezekiel looked away from the group and I knew he was still battling his demon. It was the same as mine and it had its own way of taking a hold and controlling us. "What I am saying is that just because you have a vice, doesn't mean that you let it control you. We have to work to control our carnal urges because we are flesh and we have this body, not the new body that is promised to us when we die and see Jesus on that other side."

"But I don't get it though because sometimes, I pray. I ask God to take away my desires for alcohol and I might not drink that day but give me two or three days and I'm lit."

Images of Faith and I about to fornicate passed through my eye. I could feel Satan pointing at me before the Lord and saying, "look at what Donte did." Even though my vice wasn't the same as Abednego's, I definitely identified with that inner struggle.

"You have to keep praying," Rahliem answered, "but it is good that you are honest because if you can't be honest about your sins and what you need help with, you can't ask God to help you. You pray for the strength to conquer your demons and each day you do, you thank God for allowing you to beat that demon that day. It's been a few weeks since I got high. I'm not saying that I won't get high tomorrow, but I am saying that I will praise God that I kicked the urge to get me a dime-bag for another day. I will praise God that I walked past the guy smoking on the stoop or his car or I said no to a house party and I turned to my Bible. I even thank God when I remember to keep my fingernails trimmed because I can't smoke weed the same with the nails cut than I can when they are long."

Light chuckles filled the air as I and other members continued eating and listening to Rahliem. I had a new respect for him because he was man enough to show us his flaws—inner struggles, not just perceived outward appearances. It also reminded me that indirectly, Rahliem was asking us to pray that he'd win the fight with his demon that day.

Just A Little Talk With Jesus

Malachai had blessed us with his presence for our accounting study group. I didn't know how he expected to pass the class with him showing up every now and then, but I would let him worry about that. In his defense, this was an evening class and he had a lot of meetings dealing with the university during this time. Aaliyah agreed to tutor us, her "unworthy subjects." She was the only one in our group that understood most of the concepts that was taught to us this semester and she had the B-average to prove it. As we took our seats at the tables and she stood at the tripod with the dry-erase board in front, she had a smile on her face as long as the Mississippi River.

I had taken some of the final exams already this week alone and I felt good that my studies were not a waste. I managed to balance campaigning and learning more about student leadership with ministry and the balance seemed good. I thank God for that. Earlier, I was on the phone with Elicia reconfirming appointments she had over the holiday. She had given me a good progress report about Mary's plans for expansion in Japan. When she asked about Faith, I admitted that we hadn't talked since she left a few nights ago. I tried to call her a few times, but I'd get a dial tone.

Aaliyah was trying to rush us through the concepts and expected us to grasp everything the moment the words flew from her mouth. I had suspected that perhaps she and Malachai had made plans for after the study session.

Ezekiel and Malachai were trying to get her to slow down, but that just encouraged Aaliyah to speed things up. She was ticking me off because I really needed to digest this information so that I could be armed and prepared and if I was going to struggle, I could've done this by myself. Malachai's cell went off and her smile quickly turned into a frown. As he answered the phone and then went out of the room, her face stayed that way until he got off the phone. When Malachai was done, he made the mistake of placing the phone on the table, she reached for his cell phone and Malachai didn't reach for it fast enough.

"Come on Aaliyah, you know I got a meeting in thirty minutes and I really need this study session." He pouted as he held his hand out for Aaliyah to give him the phone back.

Aaliyah scrolled through his calls and then she stuffed his phone in his hand. "I'm just making sure that girl wasn't calling you."

Well, Donlynne wasn't calling him—she was knocking on the door. She had the suit he needed to change into in one hand and his bag of personal grooming materials in another. The expression on Aaliyah's face showed resentment and she didn't mind sharing it with those whom were in the group she was tutoring.

"Relax, he keeps an extra suit in the office," Donlynne defended herself. I guess she was rightfully annoyed at the idea of being scrutinized in front of everyone.

"I know that!" Aaliyah replied sternly. Donlynne put her hand up, paused, shook her head and walked away.

"If she weren't in her 'nalia I'd smack the—"Aaliyah stormed to the door, looking to pick a fight.

"Why don't we go on a break?" Malachai suggested as he jumped up and wrapped his arms around her waist and pulling her away from the door. He grabbed his suit and they walked out of the door. Ezekiel looked at me and shook his head.

"You think they are coming back?" I asked. I really needed help because I understood some of the concepts, but I had problems applying the equations to the problem. Ezekiel always had been better at reading things and being organized, but there was a part that we both were missing.

"They're coming back," he replied with confidence, "at least Malachai will. We still got a lot to learn."

"I know that's right."

They weren't gone five minutes before Malachai knocked on the door and came in. He was wearing the navy blue suit that Donlynne brought over. He pulled his book out and we continued studying. Aaliyah never came back to help us study, but between the three of us, we were able to grasp some of the concepts. After we were done studying, Malachai invited us to his suite for Chinese food. There was a time when I had to quit eating Chinese food after my first year on campus because the delivery man used to come every day and I used to eat it every day. I just got tired of it. After he placed his order, there was a knock on the door. I knew the Chinese people couldn't have gotten here that fast.

"Sup Ezekiel," I heard Arnie say in that stereotypical southern drawl. He looked at us and nodded, "Malachai, Donte."

We gave Arnie a pound before he took a seat and picked up one of our text books.

"What are y'all working on?"

Ezekiel explained the problem to him better than I could. Then Arnie started working problems and breaking it down for us. The food came and Malachai took out some paper plates so that Arnie could share our food. Once we were finished studying, Arnie and Ezekiel and I started going over "End of Semester" reports for his presentation in January.

Christmas Break - This Christmas

*E*veryone was rushing from store to store trying to buy gifts for their family and friends. Elicia and I were rushing from beautician to M.Walker's to photographer as we had two photo shoots scheduled during the break. The pictures we were taking were being used for the posters and flyers we were making for her campaign. Elicia got her grades a week ago. Her GPA had risen to a 3.44, confirming her eligibility to pursue the crown.

I had tried to get in touch with Faith to check on her and to see how she was doing. It seemed like every time I wanted to talk to her, her phone went straight to voice mail. If I didn't know better, I'd say she was avoiding me. I apologized for letting my lust run wild but she wasn't trying to hear that, I guess.

As my focus was drawn back to Elicia, I noticed that she decided to go with the natural look for her makeup, wearing a set of browns for eye shadows, a light golden brown lip candy and a natural blush. She wore a black business suit with a matching hat, giving her that southern charm. For her theme, we had decided that she would remake Aaliyah's "If Your Girl Only Knew" video. These shots were mainly for the website that would list her platform, biography and other important aspects of her campaign.

After her photo shoot, we rushed downtown to Sweet Potatoes so we could enjoy our lunch. We were served by a waiter who was wearing a black polo and dark pants. The restaurant was dark, save for the candles floating in glass all over, which brought out the orange and teal walls that played a background to a wide variety of forties and fifties style paintings. The prints of Sarah Vaughn, Duke Ellington and Thomas Dorsey seemed to move their lips as the songs were playing in the background. There, we met with Jalail Stevens, a vice president of M.Walker's. Jalail's cornrows were reminiscent of Allen Iverson and his turtle-neck and slacks was an alternative to the dress that one would expect for a corporate level executive.

"Your mother was right. Champaign does look good on you."

I shouldn't have been surprised that Jalail would know the shade of eye shadow that she was wearing. He probably could count the number of products that were on her face. Jalail was close to thirty and married with three children. The platinum wedding ring he wore matched the band that was holding the diamond earring in his ear. If it weren't for his M.Walker briefcase, one could have easily assumed he was a rapper or a drug dealer.

"Elicia told me you made a transformation but, man, she didn't say you made a 180."

Jalail looked like he could have been a model—wait, I take that back, he was one for M.Walker back in the day.

"Yep. I've made some positive changes in my life."

He nodded his head and he continued his conversation with Elicia. We looked at the pictures from the photo shoot. We still needed to get them to a scanner, but I was happy to have the negatives and the prints. Jalail was ooing and awing over the pictures as they did turn out nice. Elicia even bared a slight resemblance to Chilli and Left Eye in some of them.

"We may be able to use one of these pictures for our upcoming catalogue." Jalail commented. The waiter came for the bill and Jalail pulled out his M.Walker's Black American Express card. I started to chip in but he gave me the look that suggested he'd be offended if I did. When the waiter left with his card and tab, Jalail pulled out a check for $1000 and passed it to Elicia. "Just give us a copy of the receipts for the photo shoot, stylist and for the website."

That's what's up. I wasn't even expecting Elicia to have gotten her sponsor so soon. We talked a little while and when the waiter came back, we grabbed our things and left. Jalail walked with us to my car and I let Elicia in the passenger's car.

"You don't have no more videos?" Jalail asked me.

"Naw man. I gave all that up. Everything I did was released."

"My wife and I used to watch your work."

I felt weird talking to a grown man about my movies. Even when I was doing them, it just felt odd. I used to have a fan base that was married who'd fallen in love with a series of videos I did with a woman whom I pretended to be married to. I was one of the first to make being "married" a big genre in that regard—now I looked forward to the days when I could find my wife and put a ring on her finger.

"But I'm glad to see you turned your life around, for real," he said when he gave me a pound, "be sure to take care of my little cousin.

"No doubt."

Jalail slipped me his card and an envelope that I pushed into my pocket. I opened the door and slipped in the car.

"Jalail didn't ask you for an autograph did he?"

I was shocked. I knew the girl couldn't hear our conversation through the car, "Naw, he just gave me an idea I could use for the campaign," thou shall not lie, but I did. I wasn't going to throw him under the bus.

"I bet." She knew I was lying. "He has been trying to get your autograph forever. He sells autographed memorabilia on the side on eBay."

I laughed at the thought of one of my autographed videos being in his collection of memorabilia. Then for a minute the thought crossed my mind as to how much one of my autographed videos would go for. I quickly replaced that thought with the amount it cost for Elicia's website to get done.

"You got that endorsement without me," I made reference to the check that M.Walker gave to her.

"Now you know that M.Walker wasn't going to pass on the opportunity to use me to promote their makeup line. Plus, one of the pictures will be used to promote their natural makeup set."

"That's what's up. We're going to Bank of America right?"

"Yep."

I drove to the bank. Elicia and I had decided to treat her campaign like a business. She opened a separate account in her name and put me on as a co-owner. This way, I could write the checks and take care of the vendors and stuff. With her now having a different account for the campaign, all the expenses that were taken out of this account and all donations were put in this account. With the exception of the photo shoot and makeup, everything would be on one statement. When we were done with the bank, I dropped her off so that we could enjoy the holiday.

New Years Eve Watch Night - Go Tell It On the Mountain

T watched as men, women and children of all ages walked into Grace United Methodist Church's sanctuary for a special Watch Night Service. I, along with the other members of the Street Disciples Ministry, agreed to serve as ushers.

This was my first Watch Night Service and I was surprised to see the church packed on a Tuesday night, but I was excited at the same time. Usually, when folks thought of New Year's celebrations, folks gathered at a home or a public place, passed along glasses of wine and ate appetizers and then watched whatever show had a countdown and they counted with the people on television.

One thing I noticed was different was that everyone wore blue jeans and some type of black boots. The members of the Street Disciples Ministry wore black ties and white button up shirts under black sweaters. Everyone else had on an array of colorful sweaters or long sleeve shirts. This was a far cry from the tailored suits, skirts, heels and hats people usually wore on Sunday. Pastor Franklin came in wearing a Kangol hat and a dark green vest over a light blue shirt and dark blue tie. He, too, wore dark blue jeans that were cuffed and some brand new Timberlands. His sand and sable hair color was kinky and rough, but contrasted with his butterscotch skin tone, easily identifying his mixed heritage. His ring finger was home to a brand new platinum wedding band and the biracial woman whom now was the first lady of the church took her place on the end corner of the first pew on the left side of the church.

The choir came in singing "Hark! The Herald the Angels Sing" giving the church a Christmas feel. When I listened to the lyrics, I realized the song could be sung any time of year. After a brief call to worship, the choir sang "Hush! Somebody's Calling My Name." Everyone who was in the church who knew the words sang along. I couldn't believe that after a year, I still didn't know all the words to all the popular church hymns and songs. I just moved along with the movement and swaying of everyone in the pews.

"Welcome to Grace United Methodist Church's 2002-2003 Watch Night." Pastor Franklin welcomed the congregation and visitors. "Tonight, is not a regular church service—we are going to do more than testify about how good the Lord has been to us. We are going praise and worship him in song and in truth. As we enter the year 2003, I want all of you to be safe when you leave the church tonight." Everyone clapped and followed the pastor's nonverbal cue to take a seat. "If you would pull out your swords, I want you to turn to Matthew 26 verse 41. If you have it say Amen, if you don't, say wait a minute."

A chorus of "Amens" and "Wait a minutes" rang the air as people pulled out their Bibles or reached under the pews in front of them for the church's Bibles and followed the command of the pastor. Once the page shuffling decreased, Pastor Franklin continued. "The Word says, *Watch and pray, lest you enter into temptation. The spirit indeed is willing, but the flesh is weak.* And a supporting verse to that is in Luke 21 verse 36, *Watch therefore, and pray always that you may be counted worthy to escape all these things that will come to pass, and to stand before the Son of Man.*

"This, my brothers and sisters in Christ, is the true meaning of Watch Night, we watch the old year go out and the new year, come in. And we pray that we are better saints this coming year, than we were last year. We are to do as commanded.

"There's nothing wrong with having fun and fellowship with believers and friends. But be careful of that definition of fun. Ephesians 6 verses 17 – 19 state: *And take the helmet of salvation, and the sword of the Spirit, which is the word of God; praying always with all prayer and supplication in the Spirit, being watchful to this end with all perseverance and supplication for all the saints—and for me, that utterance may be given to me, that I may open my mouth boldly to make known the mystery of the gospel.*

"If you know the gospel, then you know the definition of fun does not include drinking to the point where you lose your mind and have no control of your bodily functions. You know that fun is not in shacking up with someone who does not belong to you as if you were husband and wife. You know that the Ten Commandments are to be honored now just as they were to be honored when they were given to Moses on Mount Sinai.

"So tonight, in a closing of a short sermon," Pastor Franklin made room for a few chuckles as he's known to be long winded. "I want to remind you that it is important to begin and end all things with the Lord as he has commanded you to do. Keep the Holy Spirit with you as you work to make it throughout tonight and the rest of 2003 and all of the years you have here on earth."

A short clap was heard and Pastor Franklin invited any visitors who didn't know the Lord to come and receive salvation. Disappointingly, no one walked up but I trusted that every soul, including my own, was at peace with where they stood with the Lord.

A few members testified about big accomplishments that were achieved over the past year; births of first born children and grandchildren, graduations, wedding, engagements, successful surgeries and such. Mrs. Edmonds sang a soul-stirring rendition of "How I Got Over" that felt like Aretha Franklin had stopped by and made a trip. Ezekiel's rendition of "Bridge Over Troubled Waters" brought tears to my eyes as I thought about all I had overcome and the work I still had to do. Elicia and Mary sang "I Was Born to Sing the Gospel" and everyone was on their hands and feet and moving around the church in prayer and thanksgiving.

A few more testimonies were given and after an older man sang "I Don't Feel No Ways Tired" we were called to get ready for communion. Rahliem and Abednego helped Pastor Franklin set up the altar for communion. I, along with the other ushers took communion first and then we helped the congregation move through the process. The choir was served next and Rahliem and Abednego walked with Pastor Franklin to deliver communion to the elderly and those who were unable to walk to the altar. After everyone else was served, Pastor Franklin took his communion and then he looked at his watch.

"The time is now 11:57, and as we enter this New Year, brothers and sisters, I want to encourage you to continue to watch and pray and listen to the discernment in of the Holy Spirit."

Another chorus of Amens rang through the congregation as the choir sang "Total Praise." By time the choir got to singing Amen, we could hear firecrackers and explosives going off as well as bells ringing. The year 2003 was officially upon us.

Spring 2003

Be Still, God Will Fight Your Battles

*E*licia, Aaliyah and Gabrielle were getting things together for their sorority's founders' day. Her chapter was doing a presentation commemorating the founders of their sorority later on that evening. In the meantime, I was hanging out with Ezekiel, Arnez and the rest of the members of their fraternity. Their founder's day was about a week and a half ago. We were in the auditorium, waiting on the presentations to begin. A line full of young women dressed in their Sunday's best was wrapped along the stairwell leading to the entrance to the auditorium. Donlynne and some of her sorority sisters were in the back, holding balloons and roses bearing Elicia's sorority's colors. Arnisha and her court arrived too and they were having a conversation in the back as well. Arnez and members of his fraternity arrived carrying a big ole cake, trying to make their way to the front. Alumni members of various fraternities and sororities, as well as some of the faculty and staff were arriving as well.

Elicia and another member of the organization opened their doors and Monica and members of AGF were arriving in the auditorium. Aaliyah came outside to attend to some of the commotion that was beginning to form. The members of AGF were silent as Aaliyah and another member of the sorority walked down the line and then walked back up. Gabrielle and another member were talking to their alumni members as people were coming in.

The first two rows were reserved for members of the sorority. Everyone else sat behind them.

Gabrielle welcomed everyone to the founders' day. There, they gave the history of their sorority, their founders' biographies and their chapter's information. Aaliyah gave a presentation of famous members of the organization. As they were getting ready to sing their hymn, the members of AGF got up and started singing "Lift Every Voice and Sing." At first the members of the sorority had paused as the attention had shifted from them to AGF. When AGF had finished, the members of the sorority started their hymn over. Then Monica broke out and started singing "Respect," not showing them any. Aaliyah cut her eyes and started to make her way to the back. Donlynne stood up and walked to where AGF was at and asked them to leave. She pulled out her cell phone and within a few minutes, campus police were entering the auditorium. The members of AGF continued to sing until they were escorted out of the ceremony. The sorority started their song over and when they finished, everyone had clapped. Each of the other organizations presented them with gifts. Elicia invited everyone to food and closed the ceremony. I waited until Elicia and her sorority sisters were finished and then I was able to pull her to the side. She was talking to Donlynne, who had followed her to tell her something.

"I don't know why you let them come into your ceremony like that. When we had our founder's day, we didn't let them hoods in. Older sorors were not having it," I heard Donlynne say.

"We are not rude to turn guests that way. And the only reason Monica acts that way was because she couldn't get in," Elicia said politely.

"When are we going to talk about my campaign plans?" Donlynne pressed. "I would love for you to serve as my campaign manager."

"I can't, I've already made a commitment for the elections."

"Girl, you don't know what you are missing," Donlynne smiled.

Elicia and Donlynne hugged and Aaliyah walked by. Donlynne and Aaliyah exchanged looks. Elicia pulled Aaliyah away and they went to the front of the line to get their refreshments. I waited until all others were served and then I got something light and sat with Ezekiel.

"Donlynne don't know do she?" Ezekiel asked.

"I don't think so and I intend to keep it that way," I responded.

"I'm rooting for my girl," Arnie said as he sat down, "I haven't told anyone about her running. Most people who ask have speculated that they think Aaliyah is running."

Ezekiel and I let out loud laughter, as the thought of Aaliyah being Miss NC Tech with an attitude was hilarious. I didn't say too much about the campaign around Arnie because we are not supposed to be talking about it around him. He knew too much as it was about Elicia's campaign. Everyone else was talking about AGF and how rude they were. I mainly sat and listened. Mary came in briefly later on after most people began to leave. She wished Elicia and everyone else Happy Founders' Day and sat around and enjoyed the festivities.

I was surprised to see Rahliem coming in as well. I walked over to him and gave him a pound.

"I didn't know that Elicia's organization was celebrating founders' day." Rahliem said as we had gone off to the side. "Were we supposed to bring gifts or something?"

"Naw, mainly that's something the students who are in those organizations do. I'm here to support Elicia, the frats and sororities are not my thing. Plus, they wouldn't let me in anyway if I were interested." I spoke the truth. I had nothing against the organizations but I had no desire to become a member either. Even the Christian organizations were unappealing to me. But I did respect the community service they did and I enjoyed watching the step shows.

"I came up here to speak to Brothers of Christ United's Back to School Service they had in the Student Union ballroom."

"Aww man," I felt guilty because I had told Malachai that I would attend the service, not realizing it was the same day I had also committed to be at the founders' day program and the subsequent meeting with Elicia and Gabrielle on their campaign plans. "I didn't know you were speaking or I would've came."

"Don't worry about it man, the Bishop who was supposed to speak caught the flu and I was asked to come at two o'clock this afternoon. So for most of the day, I didn't know I was coming either."

Rahliem succeeded in easing my guilt. Elicia, Aaliyah and Gabrielle came up to him and gave him hugs. Ezekiel came and introduced him to Arnie and some of the other guys on campus whom Rahliem hadn't met. After a few brief conversations, members of the sorority were seen cleaning up the room and Rahliem and I made our exit.

I Shall Not Be Moved

Elicia called another meeting with her campaign team. We met at the conference room in Bluford Library at A&T. The university had so many people, if we wanted to get away, that would be where we went.

Ezekiel showed up with a few of his frat brothers and friends. Aaliyah, Gabrielle and Keisha were already wrapped up in a conversation. Some of the people who came to the first meeting were also in attendance. Elicia walked in wearing a white blouse and some jeans. A few minutes later, Mary, Arnez and a few members of her campaign were coming into the room.

Elicia and I had privately talked about the teams having a joint meeting. I was firmly against it because I felt like the intentions were good but could backfire. Elicia wanted this meeting so that the two teams could get to know each other and that there be no resentment among those who've chosen one candidate over the other. I guess I could understand it because Elicia and Mary are friends and they value their friendship and want to keep it after the race. My problem with it was that even though that was what they wanted to do, this could put the teams to believe they were mainly competing against each other.

The other effect could have been the direct opposite; everyone on our teams could have thought they had to help one another and expect to do things jointly. With this thinking other candidates could say that Mary and Elicia were running a joint campaign and only target their strategies against the two of them collectively. A candidate would see this as an opportunity to try to pit one against the other and thus ruin the friendship they are trying to preserve. I was not trying to imply that they did not have faith in their friendship. I felt that they would do better to focus on their own campaigns. Whatever these people are going to do, they are going to do it anyway so I say let them.

"We've called this meeting," Mary announced. Everyone had intermingled and taken seats, "so that we could address the issues of me and my friend, Elicia, running for the office of Miss NC Tech. Many of you are used to seeing us hanging out together and are probably surprised that we would run for the same office."

"But Mary and I both knew that we wanted to be Miss NC Tech since we were roommates at least," Elicia continued, "so we see this as a friendly competition amongst friends."

"And we want our friendship to last after the race is over with, so that means no taking down each other's fliers." Mary added.

"Or anyone else's fliers for that matter. That means no sharing campaign plans or secrets." Elicia continued.

"Because anyone caught doing so will be kicked off the campaign." Mary said.

"Most of us in this room are Christians so we need to conduct ourselves in that manner." Elicia said.

"And that means treating other candidates the way we want them to ours. That does not mean treating them like they treat us, that means treating them better. Because we are Christians, this is perfect time to let our light shine."

Everyone clapped when they were finished. They allowed for questions and answers.

"Will there be joint campaign fliers?" Keisha asked.

"The thought has crossed our mind," Mary said. "Truthfully, we will not spend our money on joint fliers because we each have different platforms. However, we know that somebody will make joint fliers spending their own money and time to do so. This is a common practice for some people to endorse a group of candidates, but it is not something individually any candidate would do."

"Why would the two of you run against each other?" Another person in the room asked.

"That's not an easy question. I'm running because it's been a dream of mine to be Miss NC Tech. I feel that I can continue the legacy that each of our previous Miss NC Tech's have left. They have used their influence to promote popular civic ideas in the community and to increase student involvement on campus," Elicia answered.

"I'm running because now is the time for the black business woman. So many of us are becoming leaders in Fortune 500 companies and running our own independent businesses. I am a fashion designer—that is no secret. I want to showcase the progressive political movement that these Miss NC Tech's have held over the years," Mary responded.

Surprisingly, no one else had any more questions. Members of our teams started talking amongst themselves while Elicia and Mary talked among themselves. Arnie tapped me on the shoulder.

"What are you doing here?" I asked because I was surprised to see him.

"I came to support my girl," Arnie responded as if that were the obvious answer. I didn't like how he said that, *my girl*. Call me a jealous ex-boyfriend if you want, but I could feel that something was up.

"I thought that current SGA officers couldn't endorse or campaign for candidates who are running?"

"I'm not. I'm just here to watch and observe that's it."

I took Arnie at his word. I didn't think he'd do anything to hurt Elicia intentionally, but I didn't want him to do anything to get her disqualified either, intentional or not.

After a few more minutes, people started leaving and pretty soon, Arnez and I were pushing chairs in.

"You got to be careful with Arnie," he warned me as I grabbed my bag to leave.

"What you mean?"

"That negro will report you to the Elections Committee and then swear up and down without hesitation that it wasn't him. Plus, he is running for President this year."

"Word?"

"Yeah, he thinks he is being secretive about it but just like everyone knows that Donlynne is running, people know he's running."

Why didn't Elicia tell me that Arnie was running for president? More importantly, why didn't *I* know about it? I seriously doubt that Elicia would join Arnie's ticket, because if she joined anyone's ticket, that would do some damage to her. How did he know about this meeting anyway?

***

Elicia and I walked to her dorm and we peeped the design for her website. We went with a black and green theme for her website and the fliers that a local student designed for us. Martin Maasai was a popular graphic artist that did a lot of fliers for Greek parties and websites for school based organizations.

"Our website has been hit way too many times," Elicia said. She had pulled up the stats from our server. "I hope that Martin didn't go around showing everyone our site."

"Does the team know you have the site or anyone in the office?"

"Only you, Martin, Aaliyah and Gabrielle know the site has been done. All of you agreed not to say anything."

"I know I haven't."

There was a hit on her guestbook that was a private message. She typed in our password and we read the note.

Aaliyah was too scared to run so you've run in her place. Well, that's too bad because I was looking forward to beating her. Be sure to tell her to stay away from my man.

There was a lot of enter spaces on the page. The further down were pictures of Malachai and Donlynne in close embraces. Then there was a phone call.

"Hello," Elicia answered. The person on the phone was talking real fast. "Hold on." Elicia put her phone down and placed it on speaker phone.

"I didn't know you went out with Donte Longstocking," that was Monica calling me out of my name.

"What are you talking about?"

"On the AGF website, there are pictures of you and Donte looking like a cute couple in our guestbook. Y'all are wearing matching South Pole outfits, you look cute."

"Hold on."

I pulled up the AGF website and went to their guestbook. Sure enough, there were pictures of Elicia and I in our youth. That day was a special day for us. I won't get into it now, but I could tell that Elicia was touched when she saw those pictures. There was a caption on the picture that asked, "Is this the Christian candidate?"

I didn't know if Elicia still had those pictures. A part of me misses those days when we were the perfect couple.

"Elicia, you still there?" Monica asked.

"Yeah, I'm still here."

"Somebody's trying to call you out, but don't worry, your secret is safe with me. We'll have our webmaster remove the pictures by 10 p.m."

"Thank you."

Elicia hung up the phone and we looked at one another. It had been a minute since we've talked about our relationship.

"Romans 5:8 says *But God proves his love for us in that while we still were sinners Christ died for us,'* " she said. I knew the verse was in Romans, I had highlighted it in my Bible. Elicia was upset and could've fooled anyone but me. *"'For one believes with the heart and so is justified, and one confesses with the mouth and so is saved,'* Which comes from Romans 10:10."

"Somebody found our old high school yearbook. I remember when our friends surprised us by purchasing the page for us," she reminisced.

"Yep, I thought we would be married by now."

"Me too."

"Then I messed it up by seeking fame and fortune. I'd be surprised if I'd get married now."

"Who's to say you won't get married? Remember, he that finds the wife find a good thing. You're supposed to be looking for her. If she comes to you then you're in trouble."

I was laughing at her attempt at humor. I looked at the pictures on the net closely. I could tell the pictures did come from our yearbook. I was trying to think who would've had access to our yearbook that would put our business out like that. My phone vibrated in my pants pocket. The unexpected sensation sent a shock to my leg.

"Donte speaking?"

"Yo, when was you gonna tell me that you and Elicia had a thing going on back in the day?" It was Malachai.

"You know I'm not with the gossip—besides, they're some pics of you and Donlynne sharing a moment on a few websites."

"For real? How recent are the pictures?"

"I don't see no date."

"I guess somebody likes to pass out pictures and forward emails and stuff."

"This is NC Tech, everybody likes to forward emails. If it isn't scandalous pictures of the candidates, then it is somebody who got the inside scoop on who they think is on line."

"I remember that year when we had a few emails floating around. Y'all haven't even turned in your packet and already somebody's starting some mess. Everybody who didn't know Elicia was running knows now. Mary's whole platform got put out on the AGF site."

"For real?"

"So where are you at?"

"On the internet," I put the phone down to tell Elicia to go the AGF site.

"Go to the news section. Somebody put her whole business out there. Pics of you and Elicia have been moved to the pictures section. Yo, hold up—those are pictures of me and Donlynne—oh snap."

I moved to the pictures section and sure enough our high school pictures were put on blast. The phone was ringing again. Elicia picked up the phone.

"I thought you were in Bluford?" Malachai asked me.

"I didn't tell you that, I'm in Elicia's room."

"That's Monica—" Elicia cut in, "put Malachai on speaker phone." I did as instructed, "Malachai guess what?"

"What's good, Elicia?"

"I'm good, Monica can you hear us?" Elicia asked.

"I'm mad yo because our site's been hacked!" Monica freaked out.

"Word," Malachai exclaimed.

"I wouldn't put y'all's business out there like that—" Monica whined, "I do a lot of things against Greeks but I keep it strictly about the Greek system and that idol worship, it's never personal."

That much might have been true. Elicia clicked to the front page of the AGF website. There was a new front page that featured pictures of Donlynne, Mary, Elicia and Monica. In the heading it said, "The Future of North Carolina Technical University is in Your Hands."

"So the secret is out." Elicia said.

"Yep, I guess it is," Monica answered. "May the best candidate win." Monica hung up the phone. Malachai hung up the phone and I grabbed my phone and Elicia's phone.

"You turn in your paperwork in three days?"

"Yep."

"Well, I guess we need to get ready for Friday."

In That Great Gittin' Up Mornin'

Friday, February 21, 2003 arrived and Elicia and I were going over this application with a fine-toothed comb. We should be alright. We'd practiced on six sheets of paper before we typed the applications to turn in. To be honest, we had a harder time locating the typewriter than we did filling out the application. It is that time of year again when everyone seems to be busy. Those who are pursuing memberships in Greek letter organizations and different honor societies were pursuing their objectives. People are also pursing titles in prominent organizations like National Society of Black Engineers (NSBE), NAACP, American Marketing Associations, New York/New Jersey and AGF. Everyone was trying to move up or move into something.

Arnie and his team were ahead of us turning in their packet. The men in black and green were excited about their upcoming campaign. Word on the street was that Arnie was expected to beat whoever his opponent would be by a landslide. Truthfully, I couldn't think of anyone who could beat him in a campaign. Donlynne and her team were behind us trying to size up the competition. They were talking about the AGF website, which to this day still had not been updated or changed. Monica and AGF had yet to gain control over their website as whoever hacked it changed all of the registration information and without the new password, they were unable to talk to the website registers to get the issue resolved. We still haven't found out who the hacker was, but that would come out eventually.

"Elicia," I heard Mary yell across the hall. I had to hand it to Mary, she looked nice in her black and pink suit that she designed. They ran toward each other and hugged tightly. I saw Arnez and a few members of her team and I acknowledged them.

"Girl, Arnie is going to be in shock when he finds out who is running against him." That comment by Mary caught a few heads as people wanted to know who was running. Then she put her hand up to Elicia's ears and Elicia had the surprised look on her face.

"You know I can't pick sides. Arnie is my friend but that is my girl. I knew she was planning something."

We saw Aaliyah and Gabrielle walking in and they hugged Elicia tightly. They were giggling with one another. Aaliyah looked at me and smiled. I had to admit that she looked good, but I knew better than to pursue this feeling. Ezekiel and some of his boys came in, too. We gave each other dap.

"I'm running for Senior Class President," he announced like he was the proud parent of the cutest newborn in the hospital.

"That's what's up. I'm glad to know our class is going to be in good hands."

"Yep, the Class of 2004 is definitely going to represent."

Our line moved forward and we were in front of a secretary. She looked over our packet and gave us the thumbs up. Elicia Edmonds was officially a candidate for Miss North Carolina Technical University. I was able to take a peek at the list. Monica had already turned in her packet. That meant Elicia would be number two on the ballot. I also saw that another woman's fliers had been confiscated with the words "applicant disqualified" written in big bold red letters. The thought crossed my mind to wonder if this was the hacker, but I decided against passing judgment on her. We showed the secretary copies of fliers we planned to make. All of our stuff had the correct time and date for the Miss North Carolina Technical University pageant. As expected, everything was approved and we waited outside.

"You're excited?" I asked Elicia. She was holding my hand and standing next to me.

"I am very excited. The race for SGA President is going to be just as good as the race for Miss NC Tech."

"For real? Who's running?"

"It's official girl," Aaliyah was forever ghetto and loud, "Gabrielle Hunter is going to be the next SGA President."

Whoa! That was going to be a tight race. Elicia works for one candidate and was line sisters with the other. Elicia and I agreed not to endorse anyone who was running for any office because we didn't want any alliance to harm our chances of winning. The fact that Gabrielle was running presented a new problem for Elicia. The fact that they were line sisters would present the illusion that they were on a ticket, but Elicia already had her own agenda. Plus their sorority would definitely be endorsing both of them together along with all the other candidates in the organization that were running. Last year, their chapter posted Arnie's campaign information along with other chapter members who were running on their site because he's a member of their brother fraternity. Nevertheless, I was happy for Gabrielle if she wanted to run for president.

***

Everyone was waiting in the lounge area again. Five o'clock could not get here fast enough. The anticipation of who was running against who was exciting. The secretary came out and she asked everyone to be quiet. Once the room was quiet, Malachai and Arnisha walked out of the office and began posting the candidate list throughout the building. That's when it became official that Elicia had four opponents: Monica Freeman; Donlynne Winston; Mary Braxton and Daisy Roxboro.

"May the best woman win," Monica was shaking our hands. I looked around and I could see Donlynne and Arnie in a deep conversation. Daisy and Ezekiel were also in talks. Elicia and Gabrielle were making their way to their organization's plot to put up some of their yard markers. The plot was an piece of land designated for a fraternity or a sorority to meet on campus. Once again it was on.

Somebody's Knockin'

y six o'clock that evening, banners, fliers and other literature for many of the candidates were already in place. I had received information on candidates, platforms, official online websites and everything else I would need. Now the real work would begin. We had a meeting with our school's Toastmaster's Club president at seven o' clock. They were hosting the first "Meet the Candidates Forum" the following Tuesday. All the candidates who wanted to participate were given an opportunity to start presenting their presentations privately and were going to receive evaluations on delivery, posture and other nuisances one could avoid when giving a public speech. Elicia and I felt that this would be the perfect opportunity to hear a public response to her campaign. We did not view this as a test run, we had decided to treat this as if this were our first official presentation.

After the filing and acceptance of our applications, Elicia and I went to CiCi's Pizza on West Market Street to celebrate. Arnie and his team were there also. Arnie was short, about an inch or two taller than Muggsy Bogues but he was built like him and about the same complexion. Elicia and I elected to sit in the back so that we could have some time to ourselves. We asked God to bless our food and began to eat. Elicia started laughing all of a sudden.

"What's so funny?"

"The way you looked when you bit into your pizza like you weren't sure whether or not you wanted to try it or not."

"I did not!"

"You should look in the mirror."

In all honesty, they had this chicken pizza that I hadn't tried before. It smelled good, but I wasn't against trying it.

"Sometimes, I worry about you," Elicia revealed, "so business-like and uptight all the time. You should loosen up."

"I am."

"See now you're lying," she chuckled again. I guess when you've dated someone for three years and been friends with them for longer than that, then you do think you know everything about them. "I want my election to be fun. I know that you are about business and that you want this campaign to be taken seriously, but you need to have a little fun. I'm not saying go to the club, drink and all that, but I want people to feel uplifted, inspired and moved when they see the people on our team."

"I am uplifting."

"You are about as stiff as the Cabbage Patch Doll on my bed at my mama's house. Been like a sick puppy since Faith left you."

"And how is she doing? I've heard you've been in contact with her."

Then she looked at me like she wanted to slap me. I had stopped calling Faith and trying to reach out to her. I figured that when the time was right for us to talk about what went down, it would come, but I wasn't going to force it either. Anyone who doesn't want to be with me or talk to me should free themselves.

"You know good and well I haven't been in touch with her. But you know she knows how to reach you when she's ready to speak with you. At any rate I am for real. I want you to loosen up a bit…but not too much. Show them a piece of the man I dated."

I looked up mid-chew and swallowed. "People have already seen a piece of the man you dated."

"Not that piece—silly. Show your charm. Smile baby. You got those LL Cool J dimples, use them. Even Jesus got to have a little fun."

I smiled involuntarily. I had forgotten that beneath this serious business woman was a kind, gentle, playful spirit that I was attracted to. I knew how to press her points too, but I wouldn't call her on it. Maybe I am uptight, but that is because even though I let everyone view my outer appearances, I kept my inner man guarded in a box.

"So answer this, if you did not make those videos, do you think we could have been married by now?" That was left field for her. I thought we agreed never to discuss our past relationship. "I got to looking at those pictures we took that were in our yearbook and some of the private ones we had and I always wondered about that."

"I don't know. I used to see visions of us being married before I did the videos—now, I don't see myself marrying anyone."

"Is it that you don't want to marry someone or are you allowing Satan to condemn you for the videos so that you don't marry the woman God has selected for you? Remember, Jesus said what God brought together, let no man put asunder."

"Didn't Mary J. Blige sing that song?"

"She did and quit changing the subject."

"I'm not. You are so interested in whom I'm marrying. What about you?"

"I don't worry about it. I don't even look because I'm not supposed to. The book says *he* that findeth the wife findeth a good thing. It didn't say nothing about asking my girls if he was the right one for me."

Before I could respond, Arnie came over to our table and sat down next to Elicia. He took a slice of our pizza and started munching on it.

"So have you decided whether you are going to endorse me or Gabrielle? It would be hot if you joined our team."

"I'm not endorsing any candidates right now. I kind of would like to stay neutral and make an informed decision when I cast my ballot."

"I can respect that, but I think you and I can build a strong ticket and do this together."

"Well, my line sister thinks the same thing," Elicia smiled. She looked past him and I turned around to see Donlynne come into CiCi's with Malachai and they had a seat next to Arnie's table. We watched as Donlynne took off her line jacket to reveal a matching green dress shirt with a button up shirt. "I see that Donlynne has made her decision to join your team."

"Elicia baby, it's not like that. Donlynne and Malachai are not going to vote against me and you know it. Besides, you are my soror."

"So is Gabrielle."

"I didn't know she was running. She didn't say nothing to nobody. Everyone knew I was running, or at least I thought they did. I thought you would have known before she turned in her application."

"I didn't know. I just received information on her platform today."

I didn't think that Arnie believed her. Truth is, I didn't think that Elicia had to defend herself. Most people know Gabrielle to be a quiet person, so it wouldn't be hard for her to keep something like this a secret from anyone. Gabrielle talked about running in the election, but she never specified what position she was interested in. She just wanted ideas on her campaign platform and what she thought would work and would be best for the students of NC Tech and that's what Elicia and I did. Arnie took another slice of pizza and left to his table. We watched as he went back and enjoyed his party. Donlynne noticed us and waved. We finished eating and later Elicia joined them for a few pictures. Something in my spirit compelled me to warn her about the photo ops that their people were taking. Yet, I said nothing. Donlynne and a few of her sorority sisters were throwing their sign as they gave a smile for the camera. Donlynne and Arnie joined Malachai for another picture. I watched as Arnie and Elicia took another picture. Even with all the family love, something still didn't seem right.

Where Could I Go

So Gabrielle and Aaliyah met with us to go to church and Aaliyah also asked about the campaign.

"I see the pictures of you and Arnie at CiCi's turned out nice," Aaliyah said.

"That quick?" Elicia asked, "I haven't seen them."

"Arnie got them posted on his website. He just changed them before we left for church this morning," Gabrielle announced, "our brothers and sisters want us to have a joint meeting to discuss future campaign plans."

I knew it had to be hard for Gabrielle and Arnie to run against each other, and even harder for Elicia. This was why I didn't want Elicia to endorse any candidate and just focus on her own campaign. Ezekiel came in a few minutes later and sat with us.

Service had already begun when Malachai, Donlynne, Arnisha and Arnie came in late. They sat in the middle of the congregation. I looked at Aaliyah and I could tell that she was not happy to see Malachai and Donlynne sitting so close together. I had my Bible and highlighter with me and focused on learning the Word. I had this bad habit of highlighting things and only reading them once or twice and then not looking at them again until someone else brought them to my attention. The pastor brought it up in his service when he said that we should bring our swords to church. I need to be looking at my Bible more. It wasn't like I didn't read other Bible verses, I just never came back to them once they were highlighted and discussed in service.

After service, Elicia, Aaliyah and Gabrielle were getting ready to go to their meeting.

"Ladies, wait up," Arnie called out to them. They waited and then they were off. Arnisha had snuck up behind me and given me a hug.

"How's the campaign?"

"It's good, it's good."

"Too bad I can't get in there and help out. I really like Elicia's platform and her personality."

"That's right, y'all can't endorse candidates while in office."

"I loved campaigning. Going around, passing out fliers, getting notes to get out of class. A lot that of was fun. But y'all hang in there, you got a solid campaign."

"Thank you."

She kissed me on my check and left. I started to go hang out with Ezekiel when Malachai approached me.

"What's good Donte?"

"Nothing man, keeping busy with this campaign stuff. Making sure everything is on key."

"Nothing wrong with that—look, I'm having a get together for a few peoples in about two weeks, the Friday after Spring Break. You think you can come?"

"I might, I got to see what my schedule looks like."

"Aight man, let me know so we can prepare for your arrival." Malachai gave me dap and went about his way. I felt a light breeze pass by me that didn't feel right. The next scent I could smell was some Liz Claiborne that let me know that Donlynne was nearby. I looked at her and she quietly turned away. I didn't know what that was about.

***

I was in the middle of going over some work for my Business Communications class when someone knocked was on the door. I really didn't want to answer the door but I felt led to get up and see the disturbance. I opened the door and Elicia walked in and sat on my bed. She kicked her shoes off and they announced their landing on the floor. She didn't look her usual upbeat self.

"Gabrielle and Arnie got into it," I didn't know if Elicia should have been telling me this. Before I could interject she continued, "Then it got personal. One attacked the other's platform. One called the other names. Then they were trying to pit brother against sister. I can't believe I wasted my time going and I'm disappointed in both of them. If I didn't feel like I was in the middle before, I know I am in the middle now, and I don't like this."

I sat down next to her and wrapped my arms around her. She rested her head on my chest. Then she continued, "I knew that running this election was going to be hard, but I didn't expect it to be *this* hard. I could deal with folks finding out that you and I used to be together, but my people fighting in public and then everyone looking at me for an answer—"

"It's not your battle Elicia. You are running against Donlynne, Monica, Daisy and Mary. If anything, I'm more concerned about your relationship with Mary."

"We're cool. We talk daily and we're still attending the Elite meetings. Donlynne showed up, but she didn't participate like she normally does. Our last meeting was tense because everyone was there except for Monica. Daisy is not a member and there are so many questions about her, who she is, and most importantly, why she's running. Our organization voted to endorse Gabrielle for president. Our publicity chair makes the announcement tomorrow, which really puts me in a tight spot because I am not endorsing anyone publicly. Yet, I am the president of the organization so I have to stand behind our organization's vote. I'm still trying to decide for myself who I want to win, but it seems like my vote is being made for me."

I didn't know what to say to comfort her. I knew this was going to be hard on her. I reached up and grabbed my Bible on the dresser. I turned to the back to look up some verses on friendship. I found Proverbs 17.17 and read the verse aloud.

"*A friend loves at all times, and kinsfolk are born to share adversity.*"

I held her tight, so that I could comfort her.

This Little Light of Mine

The Toastmasters meeting went very well. They were happy to hear Elicia's platform and were confident in her delivery. We went on to do a few dorm sweeps passing out fliers and introducing Elicia to the student body. There were also hall meetings where Elicia and other candidates discussed their platforms and interacted with the on campus residents. In between classes we passed out fliers and continued to put up posters.

In the evenings, we would study for our classes. Ezekiel kept us sane by doing Bible study with us. Mary continued to come and hang out with us every now and then. We even had a dinner party together for both of our campaign teams.

If the melancholy and the newness didn't disappear when Arnie and Gabrielle got into it after their meeting, the feeling went away when Daisy Roxboro launched her campaign. I nicknamed it the "The Daisy 'Queen B' Campaign." Remember when Lil' Kim first came out with her first album? That was what her campaign reminded me of. She had on the big black fur and this big curly wig and some hazel contacts. One flier in particular had her wearing different color wigs, just like Lil' Kim did in the "Crush On You" video. Then there was one picture of her that was over-the-top; she had on a trench coat that hung a little off her shoulder that showed a little too much skin and she was leaning back in a chair with this conceited grin on her face. I was disappointed to know that the Student Affairs office allowed the posters to be approved. That wasn't the kicker though; Daisy had launched what many would call an "anti-campaign." She picked apart every candidate's platform and brought up things about every candidate that most folks had forgotten about.

Let's start with Monica. I don't know how she did it, but she somehow obtained a copy of the application Monica had put in for Elicia's sorority during our freshman year and pictures of her at different sorority gatherings portraying her as an interest. She even got pictures of AGF interrupting Elicia's coming out show, pointing her out in the mask. Then she poses the question, "Is she anti-Greek because she couldn't get in?"

Next was the assault on Mary. She found a picture of Mary wearing a dress that she had gotten a lot of compliments on at last year's end of the year SGA banquet. Then she found a picture of Sanaa Lathan wearing an identical dress. "Original?" she questioned.

Her campaign against us was fairly good. She posted pictures of Elicia in the club with her sorority. Then she got a picture of Elicia the night of her coming out show throwing her sorority's hand sign. The caption: "Who comes first in her life, God or her sorority?" Lastly, there was a collage of me in various stages of undress in my movies with the picture of us when we were dating in the middle. The caption: "She stands by her man, even when he makes movies with other women."

But the most damaging anti-campaign was launched against Donlynne. Before I go on, I would say this was the point where I know that our Student Affairs was slipping on their campaign censoring. The first set of pictures was of Donlynne and another man kissing in a car. In the last picture, it shows Daisy smashing the car windows with a baseball bat. The caption: "What to do when you catch your girl with your man." The next poster showed Donlynne getting into it with Aaliyah at the top of the page with an arrow pointing at Aaliyah. The caption reads:

"This woman *does not* know how to handle her business." On the bottom of the page shows a picture of Donlynne getting slapped by a miscellaneous woman. The caption points to her say: "This one does." But the poster that grabbed my attention and probably the most damaging was one of her hugging or messing or being playful with fifteen different guys, including Arnie, Arnez, Ezekiel and me. The caption: "Line Name: Fifteen Ways 2 Get A-Head. Secretary of SGA by Day. Secretary of Secret Services by Night."

Looking at the posters, I remembered where I knew Daisy Roxboro from. On a personal note, *this* was the chick who I thought was following me because she wanted me again and I wanted her one time. She was fine at first, but after a while, I just wasn't that into her. Should've thought about it first, but I wasn't saved then. Daisy was a photographer on the yearbook staff and she helped with the school newspaper. That would be how she got all those pictures of everyone. As for mine, she broke a few laws to get to those pictures and if I hadn't given it up, I would have gone after her.

Elicia walked up to me as I was looking at the "Fifteen Ways 2 Get A-Head" poster.

"She does nice work to be such a mean person."

"So how do you feel?"

"If that's how she feels she got to get ahead then I say let her. She just wants to be seen and what's sad is that *this* is going to be her reward. She can't win a race that is about dignity and respect by acting ugly."

Elicia and I walked around and then we headed to our dorms. I looked back at the posters that had Elicia and I at the center. As I glanced at the other pictures around it, I'm glad she stood by me.

Completely Yes - Spring Break

Spring Break snuck upon us as we were studying for classes and campaigning. Elicia and I both took a break from the campaign and decided to enjoy our junior year on campus. In her talks with various women in student body, interest had grown in spearheading a female driving ministry group similar to the Brothers in Christ United. Some of the women had felt that they weren't properly represented in ministry on campus and they wanted a voice to mobilize young women on campus. Elicia stayed behind in Greensboro with some of her friends to help lay the groundwork for a group they called Women in the Spirit. As it turned out, one of the ladies that was in administration was a first lady to a small, nondenominational church and she had taken a liking to the idea of Women in the Spirit and agreed to help out.

Ezekiel and I agreed to work with Rahliem in firmly setting a footprint for Street Disciples in the Winston-Salem community. Rahliem had everyone meet at King Martin United Methodist Church on New Walkertown Road and he requested that everyone wear a fresh white t-shirt, black baseball caps, comfortable, loose-fitting jeans, some black and white Air Force Ones, a black backpack and some sunglasses. I didn't get the purpose of the clothes but I rolled with it because it was Rahliem's thing.

"I wonder what Rahliem is gonna have us doing," Ezekiel asked when he stepped into my white, 1999 Honda Civic. The Continental finally had its last "hoo-rah" when I arrived back in town this past Friday night and first thing Saturday morning, I went to a used car dealership and bought a gently used Honda Civic. I really wanted the Accord but the dollars weren't right and I needed to get from point A to point B. The right frame had a baseball-sized dent in it from where the previous owner ran into the back of an SUV—that's what they told me at the dealership. I looked at Ezekiel looking like an extra from a Nelly music video and I shook my head.

"I have no idea. I get that the hats, the white T's, the baggy jeans and the shoes are supposed to give us a hood edge but I don't know what we are going to do with the backpacks."

Ezekiel had moved from the dorm over the Christmas holiday. His new place wasn't too far from the US-52 Highway so I got on that and headed north to Martin Luther King Boulevard. Traffic was a little heavy for a Tuesday afternoon, but we got through it making our way to MLK in a record ten minutes. About a mile and a half away was New Walkertown Road and we could see the church that sat on a hill about a couple of blocks down from the light. We were the first to arrive at the church's parking lot and Pastor Franklin pulled up behind us in a big black van that probably could sit twelve people comfortably. Grace United Methodist Church's name and logo were on the side. Rahliem was sitting on the passenger's leaned back as if it was his van and he were driving. We got out of the car and met up with him and the Pastor.

"I can't believe Rahliem got me out here like this," Pastor Franklin said as his frayed curls rose up slightly in the wind. The short sleeve shirt revealed a unique set of body art that obviously was obtained before he found Christ.

"Man, there's nothing like getting out here and getting in front of the people." Rahliem walked beside him carrying a few packages containing *The Upper Room* Daily Devotionals as well as a community calendar from Union

Baptist Church, which was in support of the ministry. "I've talked about this for the past few months but now, we really get to be in front of the people passing out God's word and his people's testimony."

He excitedly dug into his pocket and pulled out a red pocket knife and opened the packages containing *The Upper Room*. Abednego pulled up in his Honda with an older man that bore a striking resemblance to him. I watched his golden cross gleam in the sunlight over the barber's coat he was wearing. Rahliem counted out a couple of copies of the books and then he passed them to us for us to place in our backpacks.

"Shadrach," he introduced himself to us and shook his hand. The white coat he was wearing said *Shadrach's* in fancy script with clippers hanging off the D and scissors being used for an apostrophe before the S.

"Don't y'all have a brother named Meshach?" Ezekiel asked innocently. The look between Shadrach and Abednego gave a hint that that was a subject they'd rather not discuss. "I didn't mean to start nothing, just noticed the biblical reference and figured I asked."

"Yeah, we do," Shadrach asked. "He prefers not to be called that."

"Sup Fellas," Neal yelled as if he we were standing in the middle of the football field. I could see Celtius walking beside him, wearing his sunglasses and his hat tilted low. Everyone welcomed him and Celtius as they got closer to our group. "Man, I thought I was gonna be late, waiting on this knuckle head to come."

"Don't even tell that lie," Celtius spoke, "you were the one taking forever to go through my closet to find the perfect jeans to wear. Not to mention you cleaned our Air Force Ones three times before we slipped into them."

Neal shook his head but I knew that part was true. Neal always wore street themed clothing and business attire for him was a nice button up and dark Navy or black jeans cuffed up with creases in them. "Look, if I'm gonna be out here reppin' for Jesus Christ, I'm gonna be comfortable and fresh."

That I didn't deny, aside from Rahliem, Neal was the only one out here that would rock the gear we were wearing on a regular. This ministry was gonna be perfect him.

"Well, it's not what we wear," Pastor Franklin reminded us. "It's what we are doing, which is passing out the Word of God and giving the people a chance to make an offering to the Lord."

I nodded my head in consignment of what pastor was saying and Mya pulled up in a 1988 taupe colored Mercury Cougar. A plastic shower cap covered the rollers that were still in his hair. Save for the big, cross pendant that hung from an eighties style Flavor Flav inspired rope chain, Mya looked as he were going to the ABC Store for some liquor and a chicken joint than to begin working with us. Rahliem nodded his head and passed him a stack of books. Pastor Franklin looked like he wanted to eat his words.

"Aight, fellas, the reason I got y'all out here, dressed like this, is so that we can get on the streets and meet the people. You see those two churches down the street?" I looked in the direction Rahliem was pointing in. "They've left their doors open so that you can go inside if you need to. We're wearing sunglasses not just because it's hot outside, but so Donte and Celtius don't attract a lot of attention from their fans and so that Mya can attempt to blend in with the rest of us."

Mya's scowl looked as if it wanted to two-piece Rahliem as he pressed his lips together tightly. I didn't think Rahliem had it in him to take digs at someone.

"Most importantly brothers, I want us to remember that we aren't supposed to get glory as individuals, we are supposed to allow the people to see God working in us. I know that the members of the Nation are selling their *Final*

Calls and their bean pies and y'all should try the pies, they're good for you. This isn't a completion to try to outsell them. They've been out here since the '50s and I doubt they are going to leave anytime soon. We're here to spread the Word and people will choose for themselves what they want to believe."

We followed Rahliem as we made the march from the church to the corner of MLK and New Walkertown. Elders who were going for walks, as did the few people who hung around the corner to talk trash and get their drink on had their eyes on us. One of the ladies who recognized me pulled at my arm and reached to take my glasses off, I gently tugged at her hand and placed a copy of *The Upper Room* in her hands.

"Aww, come on," she walked up beside me as we pressed forward to our destination. "Just give me five minutes."

I shook my head no and continued to keep her in my side view as we made it to the intersection and then on top of the hill that lead to the shopping center.

"Ay, y'all it's Donte Longstocking," She started yelling to anyone who would listen. Inside I felt frustrated because I really wanted to participate in this ministry and already on day one, someone, or Satan, felt determined to keep me in bondage to my past. I stopped walking as others in the group began to disperse and mingle with the vendors who had set up shop and those who were loitering around, waiting on something big to happen. "What you doing walking with this little wack group?"

The girl couldn't have been older than fifteen, sixteen tops asked as she folded her arms across her chest and she snapped her head in an attitude. Her hair appeared to be running in many directions from her head and tended to attract lint and other colorful cotton dots from her clothing or whatever she slept on.

"I'm here because we are on a mission to go out into the world and spread the Gospel of Jesus Christ."

"Jesus," She looked puzzled as if she had never heard the name before. I didn't understand how anyone who lived south of the Bible belt could be so confused. "Who is that?"

"Jesus is the Son of God—" I started to explain before she cut me off.

"How do I get hooked up with him so I could have his baby? Wonder if that will make me rich," I found it hard to believe that she was acting like a bimbo. Then I thought about how I ran from God and denied Jesus and did everything I could to keep making my movies. I took out the Bible I had placed in my backpack earlier and I reach the verses in Matthew that dealt with Jesus' birth. When I looked up, I halfway expected to the woman to run from me—I was surprised that she didn't interrupt me. Instead, I found her standing there with her mouth dropped and a few of her friends standing beside her, equally amazed.

"You want to finish the story," I felt led to offer.

Three heads shook their heads yes and I found myself letting go of my Bible. The one I had worked so hard to highlight and keep up with and bring with me to church every Sunday. The one I sometimes struggled to read at night because I ended up falling asleep at times. I gave them the Bible and the woman continued reading and from where I had ended.

"That's how you minister to people," Abednego said. "I got pulled over by this old man that used to be one of my customers and I got him to take one of the *Upper Rooms* with him."

"I didn't think I'd give away my Bible," I mentioned as we made our way to the rest of the group.

"Be glad she took it...besides, I'm sure Pastor will work it out so that you can get another one."

When I looked back at the young ladies who were engrossed in the Book of Matthew, I was glad. I felt a since of redemption as if I had undone some of the sins I probably indirectly helped her in. I was greeted by Nelly rapping about the sneakers I had on once I met with the group at the top of the hill. I looked at the man selling copies of *Winston-Salem Journal* and some of the vendors who were pushing their framed African American art and their hip hop and black history inspired t-shirts along with a young Hispanic man selling flowers and a group of young men washing cars for a fundraiser. It made me realize that the world was so much bigger than this corner and that in order for us to make an impact, we'd have to make repeated trips here and in other places for years to come.

Hush, Hush, Somebody's Calling My Name

I ended up doing another ministry event with Street Disciples the Saturday before I returned to campus. Standing on the street corners and talking to everyday people outside of the church setting made me have a new respect for the type of ministry Jesus lead. It was humbling to sell the daily devotions for a few quarters or a dollar if we could get it. When Spring Break came to an end, Elicia and I had to get back to the business of campaigning.

Our school's NSBE chapter had their own campaign forum that we were attending. Gabrielle and Arnie were the first to state their platforms and answer some questions. Both gave fiery, direct presentations that got the audience excited and captivated by their presence. Monica did her presentation next. She talked about her views on women like Erykah Badu, Jill Scott, Angie Stone and how those women were changing the perception of what beautiful should be in our community. She also went into this spill about how women should not be made to feel like they have to wear makeup or sexy clothing to make themselves look good. She then ended her presentation by singing a popular verse of Jill Scott's "A Long Walk."

Daisy looked like a biker girl with her spiked hair and leather attire. Her response to Monica's campaign was reciting the first verse of EnVogue's "Free Your Mind." Daisy went on this tirade about feminism and the movement to empower women to be stronger and more effective leaders. Daisy also went on to say that everyone should know that truth about each candidate and even revealed a few details about herself.

Elicia was up next and she talked about the legacy that the previous Miss NC Tech's have held. She went into details about preserving the past while building on the present. Elicia also talked about leadership and the impact that it has on the decisions made by organizations to do the work together or apart on campus. Finally, she talked about the importance for friendship no matter what the outcome could be.

Donlynne came and tried to pick up where Elicia left off. She also was put into a position to defend herself as a woman who knows how to get and keep her man. Daisy started to interrupt her but she was restrained by members of her own team. Donlynne closed by talking about her love for the students, her activism of student government and her family's legacy.

Mary closed by confessing her dreams and aspirations to be a fashion designer. After receiving compliments on her latest design, an African inspired business suit, she joked by mentioning that she had sent Ashanti a duplicate to wear at the upcoming *Lady of Soul Awards*. Mary's agenda was about women and minorities building strong businesses and empowering their connections, including her plans to contribute to the rebuilding of East Market Street.

To say the least, I was disappointed that Elicia had not professed her love for Jesus and how her faith kept her guarded as a virtuous woman. That was one of the thrusts of her campaign.

"They should see a virtuous woman, not hear me speak about being one all the time." She defended herself when I brought the subject up.

"But Elicia, you need to remind people that you are Christian. People are not going to get that just because you wear a cross and go to church on Sunday. What is it that you say Jesus tells people, deny me and I will deny you before my father."

"Now you know that is not what He meant," I hit a nerve and she was offended.

"I'm just saying, put Jesus in their faces. Look at Daisy, she doesn't represent you or anyone else and she is out there with it."

The minute I said that, we noticed some of her and Mary's fliers had been taken down and replaced with fliers of Mary and Elicia laughing and talking together.

They laugh in public, hard at work
All their official dates involve going to church
Claiming to profess they love the Lord
They'd rather eat cake then pick up their swords
Get what I'm saying, they claim to be friends
I'm telling you the truth, they are Lez B. Ann's

Before I could react, Mary reached up and grabbed the fliers. Tears were flying from her face as she was crying and mumbling words I could not understand. Elicia went to console her friend and was pushed away. Arnez was trying to hold her back but she was swinging at him too. Daisy was coming out of the auditorium and Mary picked up speed. Elicia was running after her because she knew that beneath all of the conceitedness, and the passion and the creativity, was a woman who was going to kick someone's tail.

"No Mary, don't do that!"

Before could Elicia could finish, Daisy's face was reacting to the force of Mary's hand making a landing. Daisy's team and Mary's team rushed to pull the two women away from one another. I picked up the flier that Mary tore down and I shook my head. Then I looked at all the pictures that Daisy had collected to create this poster attacking Mary and Elicia's friendship. Elicia was walking back to me and I crumpled up the flier and threw it on the ground.

"No weapon formed against me shall prosper," she declared as we left the auditorium. Donlynne rushed over and gave Elicia a hug. Arnie and Gabrielle also came by and apologized for the personal attack. The fact that Mary slapped Daisy had taken this election to a whole new level. I don't know if Mary and Daisy would be disqualified or how the Elections Committee was going to handle the situation. But whatever happens, this was definitely a new day.

Farther Along

On that following Friday, the Elections Committee decided to suspend both Mary and Daisy's campaign. They weren't allowed to put up new fliers; do any campaigning on their behalf or to help or endorse another campaign. Elicia and Mary haven't spoken since the NSBE campaign forum. With Daisy and Mary's fliers coming down, the other candidates rushed to take their spots. Elicia already told us that if Mary was not disqualified, she would give Mary and Daisy some of her spaces.

Malachai had invited me to a get together last week and I was getting dressed to go to that. I had felt bad for not going to the Brothers of Christ United program so I wanted to make sure that I attended this event. I hadn't told Elicia I was going, mainly because I knew she would want a break from hanging out with me all day. Plus, I needed to get away from the election drama.

I went to Malachai's suite and I knocked on the door. Malachai answered the door in his boxer shorts and a t-shirt. For a second there, I thought The Spirit might have been telling me to turn around and leave, but I wasn't sure. Plus, I didn't want to be rude so I walked in.

"I hope I didn't catch you at a bad time." I was puzzled as to why Malachai wasn't dressed if he knew I was coming. I figured that maybe I caught him in the middle of another clothing change and that he possibly wasn't going to stay due to some university business that had came up.

"Naw, Donte," Malachai assured me. I sat down on the couch and I watched a random guy and girl walk out of the bathroom. The smell of incense began to penetrate the room. "Get comfortable. I know you are tired from campaigning with Elicia all day."

I didn't know what he meant by that. I turned on the television and on BET they were advertising some rap artist's album. I looked around and I saw another barely dressed female walking out of Malachai's room. I didn't want to believe it, but I've been in this life too long not to know what kind of party this was. My flesh knew it too and it was hungry. I had been working on suppressing my urges even more since my incident with Faith but I felt like at that moment, I was going to fail. I wished I had experienced Faith for my flesh would be better prepared to tackle the women who I knew were on the other side of that door and probably all over the room. Of course, once you do it, you never forget how, but I've been out of practice for a while and even the memories of my old videos couldn't save me for what I was in for.

The dancer was shaking and gyrating everywhere all around the living room and I knew I should have left then, but I didn't. Some of the men were throwing five dollar bills in her direction. As Raphael Saadiq was singing in the background, the dancer was definitely shaking her "Body Parts." The temperature had turned up a few notches and I was just slightly uncomfortable to be here. The whole atmosphere took me back to yesterday when I used to dance like that for the ladies, when they were throwing five dollar bills at me—when that was me. The phone vibrated against my leg jolted me a little and I immediately reached for it to pick it up—just the distraction I needed.

"Hello?"

"This is Sherry from Chase and we are just calling to let you know that—" someone took my phone out of my hands.

"The star is here," the lady who had my phone said as she came and sat in my lap and she started to touch me. I saw a vision of a woman in a white veil walking down the aisle to meet me. That vision gave me the strength to get up and grab my phone. "You must be shy," the lady responded.

Next, I heard some sounds that my ears used as music and cues on what I needed to do. I shook my head and readjusted myself. Malachai and some girl were dancing out of the room and neither of them were dressed. The girl on the couch turned on the DVD player and I recognized one of the first videos I had made. My flesh wanted to stay and enjoy the party, but my soul knew that it had to go. I was fighting temptation to stay and for a minute, I thought I was going to lose. But something was dragging me out of the door.

"Donte, wait up," I heard Malachai call out after me. The girl he was dancing with was getting mad while I could see another couple taking their place.

"Look man," I said as he was pulling his boxers up. "I can't stay here. If you had caught me last year or so, I would have been willing to stay. But I'm a new man and I can't get into that."

"Aight man, I thought you would be cool with it."

"That was my past. I don't do that no more. I am not going to interrupt what you got going on, but I can't participate."

"No problem man. I didn't mean to offend you. But I got to get back to my party."

I nodded my head and I smiled at him. When he opened the door, I saw one more glimpse of my past and I let it go. I had fought temptation...and I won.

***

After leaving Malachai's suite, I headed to my own just to have my own break. I took off my clothes and jumped into the shower. Feeling the hot water and liquid soap penetrate my body, I scrubbed my body hard to take my mind off the scantily clad females and all the visions of my old videos from my mind. My body started to betray me as I could feel the blood leave my equilibrium and head in a direction I didn't want it to go. I squeezed tightly and exhaled and the temptation and the stress disappeared.

Once I finished, I dried off and walked back into the room and grabbed a clean pair of boxers and put them on along with a white t-shirt. The knocking on the door caused me to jump up quickly. I put on a pair of sweat pants that were on the floor outside of the dirty clothes hamper and I rushed to see who was outside the door. I looked through the peephole and I was surprised to see Aaliyah on the other side of the door.

"What's up?" I wasn't used to Aaliyah making a social call. I had hoped that Elicia wasn't in trouble but I also knew that Elicia had my phone number so whatever it was...

"Did you see Malachai?" Aaliyah walked in and threw her tennis star frame body on my bed. I looked at her ripped jeans and NC Tech basketball jersey with a gold undershirt, her bracelets bangle to a disappointing tune. "I've been trying to call him and when I knocked on his door, he didn't answer me."

I exhaled softly. I didn't want any drama, especially and dealing with Malachai. "I saw him. I just got in from his place. Maybe they went somewhere after I left."

Aaliyah sat up and rolled her eyes at me, as if *I* was the one at fault. "I'm sick of his games."

An un-Christ-like thought rolled across my head but I chose not to say it. I didn't know the true nature of Malachai's and Aaliyah's relationship, nor was it any of my business. I watched the tears fall from her face in slow motion and later build up to a water fall. A small lake was forming on her jersey where the drops of water congregated after falling off of her chin. I walked to her and gave her a hug because I knew that whatever problems they were facing, only Jesus could solve them and all I could do was support her as she got through the next minute.

Victory is Mine

*A*aliyah crying in my arms was unexpected. After a few minutes, she had gathered herself in the mirror and she left. It wasn't my place to tell her what I saw in Malachai's suite as I figured he had bigger issues to battle and her knowledge of them would compound on the situation and make it worse. Not only did I not share with Aaliyah what I saw, I avoided the questions that were asked by others seeking his whereabouts. What I saw gave me a greater discernment and revealed to me that he had a bigger battle to deal with and all I could do was pray for him for I knew that he had a hard road ahead of him.

Elicia was getting ready for her pageant that she was going to be in next Sunday. She had her outfits laid out on my bed. I had to take them to be cleaned on my way to Winston-Salem for the weekend. Ezekiel, Aaliyah and Gabrielle were in the room helping us get ready with the clothing. She seemed to be calm and as far as I knew, she didn't mention Malachai to Elicia or Gabrielle.

Ezekiel and I were outside in the living room area while Elicia was changing into outfits and coming outside to show us. A knock on the door led Ezekiel to get up and answer it. Malachai came into the room and took a seat next to us.

"So Mr. President, what do you have planned for the Class of 2004?" Malachai asked. He and I shared a brief glance but he looked away and down on the floor.

"Basically, my plan is to make the class proactive. Stop saying we are going to do community service and raise money for scholarships and start doing community service and raise money for scholarships. Also, I want us to take more of an active role in putting on our Spring Fest. The freshmen, sophomores and juniors will be too busy running for office and pursuing different organizations and scholarships. The seniors are getting ready for graduation but we can leave a legacy, show these underclassmen how it should be done." Ezekiel laid out what had become his promise to the Class of 2004. Since he was running unopposed, he took the time to visit with many organizations to let everyone know about the new role our class was going to have in the future of NC Tech.

"That's what's up. You will be in the SGA office a whole lot then."

"Yep."

"You know they are allowing Daisy and Mary to be in the Miss NC Tech Pageant," Malachai informed us.

"Yeah, I figured as much." I hadn't heard word of a disqualification so the news was not much of a surprise. "It will be interesting to see how they bounce back to regain votes they potentially lost."

"I'm looking forward to seeing the pageant for myself. Just to see what these ladies are going to come up with."

Ezekiel got up and answered his phone. It felt awkward being around Malachai. Elicia came out wearing this blue and white business casual attire and her hair was curly. We complimented her on her looks and she went back into my room to change into another outfit and to work on her presentations with Aaliyah and Gabrielle.

"I just wanted to make sure there was no ill will between us," Malachai said as he scooted toward me, closing the space between us.

"I don't hold grudges and I don't pass judgments. Especially since I used to do what you enjoy doing. Everyone has their thing that they got to work on."

Malachai exhaled and he stood up. I could see the troubled look on his face as he paced the living room. "I've tried, but the more I think I want to stop, the more I still do what I do. I'm having fun." He looked at me and then he looked on the floor again. "I don't think I can stop."

"Let me ask you something—are you *really* enjoying what you are doing? I know the first few minutes must be nice but what about the next five. It's like a drug and people don't always see it as a drug or as an addiction and as a result, don't feel they need to be cured from it."

My discernment had been right. What I saw in Malachai's room was part of a bigger picture that he needed help and prayer with. I knew from private conversations between us before that he mentioned the pressures and the consequences of being in leadership and he told me should I step into student leadership in a bigger role, I'd have to learn how to deal with it. Malachai had been one of my first supporters when I turned my life around and gave it to Christ and he allowed me to play a small role in helping him campaign to be student government president, it pained me to see him in his weakened state. Especially when I knew his love for the Lord was as real as mine.

"Anything that can help me stop this before I mess up my future in politics would be greatly appreciated," He appealed to me.

"Hold on," I got up and knocked on my door. Aaliyah opened it and I instructed her to bring me a red folder that was on my dresser. When she came back with the folder, I sat down next to Malachai and handed it to him. "The place is in Winston-Salem. Might be a good thing considering your relationship with everyone in the school. They are discreet, so no one should be in your business unless you want them to be."

Malachai took the papers from me and then he looked at me. "Is this a twelve step program or something?"

"Something. Look at it like this, Elicia used to tell me that anyone who wanted to be saved and come to Christ could come to Him as they were. No matter what they done or how deep their problems were, our Savior was Jehovah Raafah and he could heal all those who asked to be healed. You already took the first step, you just got to come through with the rest."

I knew about the place I was sending him because when Pastor Franklin was an associate pastor at another church, he encouraged me to seek the help of a sex counselor who would help me deal with sex addiction and leaving the life style of an adult video star behind. At first I was offended because I thought that Pastor Franklin was testing me to see whether or not I was serious about my salvation, but once I went to the first meeting, I saw that the people there not only cared about helping me turn away from the temptation to have sex, they wanted me to further my relationship with the Lord. I remembered taking classes in the day time and meeting with the counselor at night. We met all over the city at bookstores, cafes, churches and community centers where I would interact with others in the community while I found positive ways to use my time. While I didn't view what I had as a sexual addiction, I see now God's true purpose for introducing the counselor in my life. Malachai needed him, but I benefitted in having someone around who held me accountable for staying committed to the Lord and continuing the steps I was making to be a better Christian.

"Thanks man," Malachai gave me a hug and walked out of the room. He gripped Ezekiel as he was coming back inside. The fellas and I were out in the lobby, waiting on Elicia to change clothes, showing off the outfits she was wearing for the Miss NC Tech Pageant.

"That was some chick on the phone spreading a rumor about Malachai, I hung up before she could finish."

"Oh."

"Speaking of Malachai, where did he go?"

"He just came by for a minute to get some information from me. He got an appointment to be at."

"Aight, that's cool."

Elicia, Aaliyah and Gabrielle left my room and Aaliyah was trying to lock the door and I was laughing. Ezekiel saw her and was laughing.

"What y'all laughing at?" Aaliyah asked.

"Cause Donte sitting right there and you didn't think to hand him his keys for him to lock the door."

Aaliyah threw the keys and they hit me in the chest. They landed kind of hard too, but I was still laughing.

"Where's Malachai?" Aaliyah asked as she looked all over the room for him. Elicia must've told her he was outside.

"He left to get away from you," Ezekiel teased as he jumped up and Aaliyah ran after him.

"That girl needs help," Gabrielle said. Elicia nodded her head in agreement. Gabrielle stayed outside as Elicia changed back into the black jeans and the blue and white pinstriped button up that she originally wore with the loose fitting white tie with a big blue carnation in the middle. We left my room and Gabrielle and Elicia both pulled out campaign fliers that were in their purses to do some more dorm sweeps and to advertise the Miss NC Tech Pageant. We ran into Monica and her team as they were passing out fliers and promoting their annual Anti-Greek rally, which was the day before the election. The members of AGF started singing their song and reciting their chant against the Greeks. Aaliyah, Gabrielle and Elicia smiled and continued to pass out fliers, taking the high road and avoiding the confrontation that the members of that organization wanted.

Miss North Carolina Tech University Pageant - Donlynne's Legacy

he banquet hall where the Miss NC Tech University Pageant was held was a large room in the Student Union. The green, yellow and white streamers and balloons representing our school's colors were all over the tables. Outside the doors of the banquet hall, the campaign teams were passing out fliers and promoting the agendas of each candidate. Inside, each team was assigned a section where they could sit. Donlynne's side was decorated in apple green and white and our team had light blue, white and yellow streamers. Monica's team had black, red and green decorations and the first section since she was first on the ballot. Mary had green, yellow and white while Daisy had black and silver balloons highlighting their own sections.

Students and campaign members were piling into their respective sections and conversing between teams. Other election highlights and rumors of who was running for NAACP president and president of our Student Union Association were filling the room. Spring semester tended to bring about tabloid season as students progressed to gossiping about who was pledging which fraternity or sorority and which Greek-letter organization "allegedly" got suspended or what they thought was going on in someone's process. The emails that my student account got clogged with along with some of the anonymous pictures that appeared on a gossip website and message board kept everyone's focus on other people's business and I wasn't trying to hear all that blasé blasé.

The candidates were getting ready to enter the room and this was the one surprise that Elicia kept hidden from me. We went over speeches, songs, wardrobe and other alternatives but I let her plan her introduction.

Arnisha took center stage along with our Attorney General. The room got quiet and she started to dance to the African beat that was playing.

"Welcome to the Spring 2003 Miss North Carolina Technical University Pageant. I am your hostess and current Miss NC Tech, Arnisha Patterson. Our Student Government President, Malachai Watson could not make it due to a medical appointment, so let's take a moment of silence to wish him a speedy recovery."

The room paused for a minute. I had forgotten about the mid-Sunday meetings that the organization had but I see that Malachai was serious about getting help. For that, I was proud of him.

"I would like to introduce a young man you don't get to see too often. A man who spends a lot of time defending our constitution, and helping our students get back on the right path after being on academic probation. He is our Attorney General, Lionel Matthews."

The room erupted in applause as Lionel rubbed his head. I didn't see Lionel too often myself except for when he and Malachai were hanging together. In fact, he was at Malachai's get together, too. No judgment.

"Well, without further ado, we will let the candidates introduce themselves."

A man dressed in AGF military gear came out beating a drum. It took me a while, but I recognized the beat to Tony Toni Tone's "I Couldn't Keep It To Myself" melody.

"A woman of natural beauty is to be appreciated. She doesn't need makeup, a perm, fragrance or tight fitting clothes to fit American's definition of looking good. She has many talents to share," Monica spoke as she came out wearing AGF black, red and green fatigues. She had the Kenyan flag wrapped around her head with a little bit of hair sticking out. The drum beat stopped and Monica sang the chorus of India.Aire's "Brown Skin."

"Our Miss NC Tech embraces natural beauty and her brown skin. Vote for me as Miss NC Tech."

People clapped. My body tensed up as I was nervous about what Elicia had in store. When she came out, I was completely shocked. The melody to *Poetic Justice* came on and Elicia had on a white headband, a white shirt and some black pants, like Janet Jackson had on at the end of the movie. She was rocking a beaded necklace with a fish on it.

"People persecute me for my strong beliefs
They don't see the love I have for them inside of me
They think that I think I'm holier than thou
But it is to Him that I bow
So I continue this journey on my quest
To live my life and to be the best
Sarah, Ruth, Miriam and Mary
It is these strong women who encourage me to carry
And as I look forward to being your next Miss NC Tech
I will carry on."

The melody carried on and then it faded out. Everyone clapped and I was proud. This was different and she definitely was coming out of her shell. A big mirror was brought out and Donlynne walked out and stood before.

"Mirror, mirror that I see,
Who shall be Miss North Carolina Technical University?"

The mirror responded, "Only the young, gifted and wise
Will have the honor of winning this prize
Three mothers have come forth and reign supreme
This title wasn't built for princesses but for queens
Royal lineage, the best sorority and SGA dedication
But the title is yours, Miss Donlynne Analise Winston"

 A few people clapped and she took a bow. I was expecting more from her, but maybe she had something up her sleeve for later on. A tambourine started playing and a few people on Mary's team started clapping. The harmonious melody reminiscent of the Sister Act II rendition of "Joyful, Joyful" filled the air. Mary got up from the crowd and she danced her way to the front. And to my surprise, she was wearing a Baby Phat jumpsuit and singing "Joyful, Joyful" with her street team. It was a nice rendition and the audience was signing along.

 Then the music did a 180, from gospel to rock and roll. Someone with an electric guitar started playing the opening solo to Prince's "When Doves Cry." We looked for Daisy to come out but still no Daisy. Then the guitarist left and a DJ put on the instrumental to EnVogue's "Free Your Mind." A few photographers burst through the door and we could hear Daisy shouting the words to this song. Daisy was rocking an old school, eighties-style, big haired wig. She had on a tight shirt that gave away the fact that she wasn't wearing a bra. The skirt had slits on the side, emphasizing her features. Her stockings were as big as fish nets and her heels were at least two inches high. The makeup on her face was black, purple and silver and she was rocking it. She threw glitter in the air and she pretended to push a school reporter out of her way. I'm not going to lie, Daisy knew how to make a grand entrance.

Miss North Carolina Tech University Pageant - Mary's Joint

*A*fter the entrance to the pageant, the first thing on the agenda was the business attire. They were judging the style and professional appearance. Surprisingly, Donlynne was up first.

Donlynne sported the traditional NC Tech business attire, which consisted of a blouse and a skirt. She wore pearls and silver jewelry. On her left breast was the ivy leaf adorned in pearls with her sorority's letters in the middle. She credited Donna Karen for being the designer and walked off the stage.

Monica Freeman was up next. She wore a blue pinstriped suit with a matching hat. This went against her "natural woman" motto. She still looked nice. Her flat shoes accentuated her height. She credited Liz Claiborne as her designer and walked off stage.

Elicia walked on the stage next, sporting a black blazer and pink shirt with a matching black skirt. Her silver fish necklace rested on her shirt. She credited Mary Braxton for being her designer and the room applauded. I forgot that Elicia models for her part time, but it was cool that she chose her girl's design.

Daisy came out with a dark gray business suit and sporting a briefcase. Her suit was real bland, even for her tastes. The heels were moderate in height. To be Baby Phat she wasn't wearing it right.

Mary commanded the stage with a dark green, light golden striped three piece. The dark green and yellow speckled tie screamed "watch me" as it played against her yellow shirt. Surprisingly, the dark green Kangol made me think of a thin French woman. The yellow tea rose accentuated her stuff and made everyone zoom in on her chest. This was definitely her show.

Miss North Carolina Tech University Pageant - The Daisy Roxboro Show

*N*ext up was the talent portion of the pageant. This was interesting because I knew what Elicia's, Monica's and Donlynne's talents were. Mary's and Daisy's were a complete mystery to me. We were allowed a short rest break before the rest of the pageant would continue. No one was allowed to speak to the candidates until the Question and Answer portion of the pageant begin.

"Mary is winning the pageant," Aaliyah tried to whisper discreetly. I watched as Gabrielle and Arnie answered students' questions about their platforms.

"Elicia is doing good. She has made a good impression on the students. The game is not over yet; we don't know what Mary's talent is and you and I both know that Elicia has her choice of talents."

"I know. I just don't want Mary to leave the pageant as the winner because she entertained a group of students. That was what we were saying last year when Arnisha was running."

"Don't remind me. Have faith Aaliyah, Elicia will persevere."

We walked into the ballroom and the lights were dim. "Greetings, and welcome to the talent portion of the Miss North Carolina Technical University Pageant. As you have had a chance to listen to the candidates talk about their campaigns, I'm sure you have made your judgments based on their platform and what they stand for. I just wanted to remind you that you guys need to get out and vote. Just because someone wins the pageant in your eyes doesn't mean they are going to win the election unless you get out and vote. So how many of you are voting on Wednesday?"

After hearing a lot of applause from the audience, Lionel continued, "First up, we have the talented Mary Braxton."

The room applauded for her as she walked to the stage. She was wearing a fat suit and a grey wig. She had on a big purple dress.

"Y'all get somewhere and sit down," we heard her do her impression of Madea. "Y'all remember my play, *Diary of a Mad Black Woman*? I'm gonna do that play for you. Now you know I like to start my show on time—what?" She addressed someone in the crowd. "Little girl, I don't know who you are talking to but you keep on you gonna be in touch with a lot of pain, understand. Hold up, let me get my medicine."

Mary pulls out a lighter and brings a flame to the candle, "oh, don't worry, it's a birthday candle. I couldn't bring my real medicine, I had to bring the sugar pill. They'd put me in jail if I had the real thing. I don't want to go to jail y'all."

Everyone was laughing as she tried to smoke the candle, but she was unsuccessful. She walked over to where her campaign team was and put the light out on someone sitting in her seat. The person got up and ran out of the room. People in the room were laughing again.

"Y'all told me to put the light out, you didn't say I couldn't put her lights out," Mary continued to laughter, "Now where was I? For those who are Christian, please turn your Bibles to John 1:1-6. If you have it say Amen, if you don't have it say can I get it."

"Can I get it?" a deep voice yelled in the crowd.

"Oh boy you nasty, you know I *clink, clink!*" Mary said as she continued with her monologue on John 1:1-6 and how peace was made of steel. Mary definitely raised the bar on the competition with her Madea impression. She definitely had us rolling with her performance.

Next up was Daisy. She came out with a tight body suit with a cross on. She started singing Madonna's "Gonna Take You There." When she got to a breaking point, she stopped and the song was switched and people could see the glowing lines on her suit when someone pointed a light in her direction. She started performing Lil' Kim's "Human Nature" with the help of her campaign team. In her performance, she yanked off her cross and threw it in our direction. I caught it and put it in my pockets as she wasn't getting it back. Her little routine ended with a group of people doing an African inspired dance with her chanting like Lil' Kim does at the end of the song. I don't think Lil' Kim would have been happy with Daisy's interpretation of her song, but that is not for me to judge.

Monica followed next with a jazzy version of "My Love, Sweet Love" by Patti LaBelle. Throughout her show, clips of the movie and the play students did last year were showing in the background. She wore a dress just like Savannah from *Waiting to Exhale* did when she was dancing with that one guy at the dinner party. She even had a rose in her hair. She ended it by singing the second verse of Erykah Badu's "On & On," as if she were in the music video.

Donlynne was up next as she grabbed the microphone and walked through the crowd. She recited and acted out her poem "The Rock Cries Out to Us Today" by Maya Angelou. She enunciated each word. She sounded nice but I just didn't get into her performance. There was nothing special about her performance, just a nice outfit and her being able to remember the poem.

Elicia continued her *Poetic Justice* theme and sang a portion of "Again." She was rocking a curly wig that she had in the same updo Janet had in her video. She was writing the lyrics of the words on a projector. Just when she was getting ready to get to the chorus, a DJ started spinning "Notorious" by P. Diddy. She looked up like something was wrong and kept singing and writing. People were chuckling in the crowd because they knew she didn't listen to rap music. Then the DJ played "Forever Always," by Monica. Elicia started singing along with it, too. I kept looking at the DJ trying to figure out what it was. Then "Doin' It" by LL Cool J started playing. Everyone in the crowd was shocked and I heard a few people snicker. Elicia got up and put on a baseball jersey and a matching hat and grabbed the mic and started singing "Shackles" by Mary Mary over the LL Cool J beat. Elicia pulled off the Mary J. Blige look from her "Real Love" video. The crowd got excited and everyone was clapping their hands. I knew about the Mary Mary/LL Cool J mix but all the stuff before it was definitely not in the script. The DJ cut part of the melody in the LL song for each very but when Elicia flowed over the beat, it fit like a glove. I was proud of her though because she put together a wonderful performance and kept the audience entertained. I looked over toward Aaliyah and I'm sure that any concerns about Elicia's performance and ability to entertain the student body were silenced. I was proud that my girl was doing her thing.

Miss North Carolina Tech University Pageant - Monica's True Desire

"Give those wonderful ladies a hand," Arnisha commanded. One of the guys from Daisy's camp came over to where we were sitting.

"Aye, have y'all seen the cross necklace Daisy threw over here?"

I wanted to lie so bad and be like "no" but I didn't say anything. I felt the Spirit directing me to take the necklace out of my pocket and hand it to him. I didn't want to do it but I did so to please Him.

"Thank you. I didn't know that she was going to throw the necklace at y'all, or else I wouldn't have let her borrow it," the guy told me. He tried to put the necklace on, but the clasp was broken. "I can't believe she broke my chain. Let me roll with y'all for the rest of the evening."

"No problem," I got up and offered my seat to him. I stood up and walked to the side as Daisy got up to answer the first question.

"These questions are personal, as I have been watching you young ladies throughout your campaign. Although I can't endorse one candidate over another, I encourage you to think about your words and your actions in the next three days. Daisy you are up first."

Daisy walked to the stage wearing a white t-shirt and some jeans. This was one portion of the pageant where they were allowed to relax a little bit.

"If there was one thing you could change about your campaign strategy, what would it be and why?" Arnisha challenged.

Without missing a beat Daisy replied, "I would have done some video footage of each of the candidates. Pictures only tell part of the truth, with video footage everyone could see a clear picture. Some of the footage I have I can't show because the rating is higher than R, but other than that, I thought everything was cool." Daisy looked at me and walked back to her seat. The thought crossed my mind to remind her that she was in one but I kept that comment to myself.

"Thank you Daisy. Next up we have Donlynne." Arnisha continued. Donlynne walked to the stage wearing her SGA uniform. "If legacy weren't a factor, what title would you pursue other than Miss North Carolina Technical University?"

"I'm not going to lie, I do feel some pressure to win Miss North Carolina Technical University, but I would pursue the Public Relations title. I like to be seen and heard and I love the opportunity to let the world know that North Carolina Technical University has always and still is doing wonderful things." Donlynne returned to her seat near her campaign team. That was the best performance she'd given throughout the pageant.

Arnisha continued, "Thank you. Elicia you are next." Elicia goes up wearing her Sunday best, a purple business suit with a purple and gold hat with a black trim. "Let's pretend for a second that Jesus was not real. How would you live your life?"

"I once heard a man say, 'I would rather live my life as if Jesus were real and die to find out that He was not, than to live my life as if Jesus does not exist, then die to find out that He is.' That's my inspiration to do right." Elicia walked off the stage confidently and took a stand next to me. I felt good knowing that she gave an answer that surely made Jesus proud.

"Thank you Elicia. Mary you are next." Mary was wearing a green gown with sleeves that had the back cut out. On the front she had her logo across the chest, "now, I'm about to put someone on the spot. When Elicia announced that she picked Donte Speaks as her campaign manager, everyone and their mom had something to say. Everyone's talked a lot about my friend and I know some of y'all got a collection of his videos. So, I want you, Mary, to give him a complete makeover. Tell us, what would he look like after you designed a banging outfit for him?"

Everyone in the crowed was laughing at me. I knew there would be some shots made at me so I took it in stride.

"First, I'd have him put in some draws; I'll be nice and say some boxer briefs."

They are trying to clown. That ain't even kosher. Everyone was oohing and ahhing and I knew good and well that they could picture me in some boxer briers.

"Then I would allow him to wear a form fitting t-shirt since he likes to show off a bit. Then he would wear a white button up shirt with a silver and black tie. I would design a three piece complete with a four button up jacket and slacks. To top it off, I would find a nice silver and black Kangol hat. He would have the look of a sophisticated, yet stylish, young business professional."

"Thank you, Mary," Arnisha winked at me. She was going to get it after this program was over with. "Last but not least, Monica." Monica walked up with a flower on her left side and her hair in a bun. She had on an African dress. "If you had to pledge a sorority, which one and why?"

A bunch of "no she didn't" and "she went there" among other comments filled the room. Monica exhaled and started, "I would take the initiative to create my own sorority. I would create one where strong black women are trendsetters and creating legacy's not resting on them. I would want a sorority that did not take into consideration what you looked like or how much money your mama had. And last but not least, you wouldn't be able to get in because your mother, sister, grandmother, step mother or whoever is a member. You would have to work your way in...calling nationals wouldn't be an option because either you have what it takes or you don't." A bunch of oohs and aahs went in the air and all I could think about were those pictures Daisy put up.

Miss North Carolina Tech University Pageant - Elicia's Test

*A*fter the pageant was over with, the candidates' returned to their teams. Elicia and Mary were answering questions from prospective voters. I felt good about Elicia's overall performance. I think that she and Mary made the best cases for why they should be Miss NC Tech. Donlynne should have come stronger and I was very surprised at the lack of organization she appeared to have. Monica was alright, but she didn't impress me. To me, Daisy showed everyone why she should not be Miss NC Tech.

"Thanks for letting me sit here with you," I looked at the man who had on his Daisy Roxboro campaign shirt. He took it off, "I'm about to give this back to her. I can't roll with her no more."

"Well, do what you have to," I told him. I watched him go and give a member of their campaign team his shirt. He walked back up to me and shook my hand. His hand shake was limp and something in his demeanor spoke of femininity. I made an effort to avoid judgment. "I'm Eric." He responded lightly when he looked into my eyes. "You may not like what I am about, but I like how Elicia is genuine in her walk with Christ. I can tell by the team she's assembled."

Now that the light was on, I was trying to figure out where I would know Eric from. It didn't dawn on me then, but I figured I would remember him from somewhere.

Elicia came back and gave me a hug. "I'm proud of you." I told her. When she let go, I could see a smile on her face. Aaliyah and Gabrielle and other members of her sorority ran up to hug her. I hadn't seen Keisha in a long time, but I hugged her when she walked to me.

"I got my own Bible now," she replied and I smiled. It was good to know that she remembered me for something else other than my video. Ezekiel and some of his brothers walked up and gave me a pound.

"Y'all did good! It's gonna be a close race between Elicia and Mary," he told me.

"I feel that way, too," I responded to him. Monica and AGF walked past us. She looked like she had an attitude on her face. I let the fact that she didn't say excuse me and that she stepped on my toe slide. It's not my fault she didn't bring her A-game. I looked over to where the executive board was sitting and I see Arnisha, Lionel and Donlynne talking. The cell phone I had was vibrating and I looked down and seen a message from Malachai.

Thanks for the tip. I hope all went well for Elicia

"Malachai says he's doing fine," I told Arnisha as she gave me a hug. She took my phone from me and read the message.

"He's not supposed to be wishing no one luck—but he chose a good one." Arnisha hugged the rest of our team and Donlynne was being cordial and shook our hands. Elicia and Mary continued to talk to other students. I felt a tap on the shoulder and was surprised at who I seen when I turned around.

"Faith?"

I couldn't believe that the woman who was standing in front of me was a few pounds lighter and probably an inch taller than when I saw her last. Here I had been calling her every day during the last week of our exams and the first week we came back from Winter Break. I took Elicia and Rahliem's advice to let her go and focus more on God. Now she was standing before me and my heart fluttered and flashed as I breathed in her lavender and mango fragrance. She gave me a quick hug and then took a step back.

"It's good to see you, Donte," Faith looked me in the eyes. She still had a wide smile and I was content with the fact that I had something to do with placing it on her face.

"It's good to see you, too. How have you been?" I had a bunch of questions like 'why didn't you return my phone calls?', 'do you forgive me for putting pressure on you?', 'are we still cool?' My lips wanted to speak but I willed them to stay quiet.

Faith exhaled. "Tax season has been working a sistah's nerves, I tell you. But I love the work I'm doing at the office helping people understand their tax returns and helping them find credits and deductions so they can get refunds." I remember Faith telling me about getting an internship to do taxes and work in an accounting office. I didn't remember her saying that she would be gone most of the Spring semester though.

"I didn't know you did taxes," I suggested as I looked to see where Elicia was at. I didn't locate her, "I'd have you do mine."

"I took the internship so I can gain business experience working in an office. I eventually want to have my own accounting firm working with small business owners. What better way to meet potential customers than to work in a tax firm?"

"You are right about that. Anyway, you need strong internships as well as good grades to get a good job upon graduation."

"And you need to know people and not burn any bridges—" she paused. For a moment I thought something was wrong. "I guess I didn't do a good job of saying goodbye." I took that to be her way of saying 'I'm sorry.' We both owed each other an apology.

"Don't worry about it. It was my fault for coming on too strong and for putting you in a position where you had to make a judgment call."

"Well if I remember correctly, it takes two to tango." I didn't expect Faith to take any ownership or responsibility of what happened that night. "I had already seen the movie and when I saw the real thing, I couldn't handle it." She laughed and shrugged it off. "I started looking for cameras and waiting on the director to say 'cut!'"

I laughed with her. I could understand her hesitancy. "I don't even own a video camera anymore."

"I bet you wish you had one to record Elicia's performance." After I shook my head in confirmation she continued, "I wish her and Mary the best. I hope that either of them win and represent your university well."

"I believe they will."

"Well," she readjusted her purse over her dark blue suit. "I need to be going now. Maybe I'll see you at T sometime?"

"Maybe."

She gave me a hug and then I watched her walk out of the banquet hall. I was happy to see her and felt like I could finally close the chapter I shared with her in my life and move on. I wouldn't have a choice because I still had a campaign to manage and Elicia and Mary just turned up the heat. Three more days before the election and the race just stepped up a notch. Maybe that would be all I would need to forget about her and focus my energies elsewhere.

Standin' in the Need of Prayer

unday night and Monday were filled with dorm sweeps, hall meetings and class. Elicia and I seemed to be going round and round in circles with the dorm meetings, club meetings and our already hectic class schedule up to the day before elections.

Since Tuesday was the day before the election, all of the candidates were required to attend all of their classes. Anyone reported absent without a doctor's note risked being disqualified. The candidates, campaign managers and official staff members were also required to attend the final forum for the class officers and the debate for the executive officers. Tensions were high as the candidates passionately stated the positions, went after any student who appeared undecided and reminded students why they were the perfect leaders for the student government positions. After the forums there was a banquet held for all the candidates.

Donlynne and Arnie were thick as thieves. They clung together tighter than a man and his woman heading out of the sanctuary after being pronounced husband and wife. Dressed alike in black suits and green shirts with green and yellow ties, they made it official that they were trying to be a ticket. Gabrielle, Elicia and Mary had their teams hanging out together. All three of them were wearing semi-formal blouses and slacks and their sections were decorated in baby blue and pink. AGF had a section for Monica and other AGF candidates who were running for various offices. The current executive board members had their table. Everyone was hanging out and having fun, moving from one table to another as they sought to mingle with the candidates and everyone continued to push for those last votes.

"I should get you to wear one of my designs," Mary said as I gave her a hug, "I already got Elicia modeling my stuff, I could put you on, too. Give you a new start."

Wasn't a bad proposal. Give me a chance to be a model of a different kind—worth giving it a shot. "I'll think about it." I didn't know whether or not that was something God would permit me to do again, being in front of the camera. I was going to pray about it because I had a part of me that wanted to do it and a part of me that had concerns about whether I was strong enough spiritually to withstand the temptations that came with modeling.

"What are y'all over here planning?" Elicia walked up to us, putting down her plate of refreshments.

"Nothing," Mary responded, "I'm trying to get models for my men's line. We start showing off our fall line soon and I'm trying to put as many students on as possible."

"That's what's up," I responded as Arnisha and Malachai were walking around delivering pizzas to each candidate's station. We were enjoying the repast. I got to see the different placards people made. Naturally, a lot of Elicia and Gabrielle's sorority sisters were walking around with placards endorsing the two candidates. A lot of Arnie's brothers were walking around with placards for either Arnie and Elicia, Arnie and Mary or Arnie and Donlynne. Donlynne's sorority sisters had placards for her and Arnie. My favorite one was the ones that were made for Mary and Elicia stating that between the two, Miss NC Tech was in good hands. Ezekiel had on placards for Elicia and himself. AGF produced their own placards for all their candidates and they were encouraging folks to write in a non-Greek candidate.

Daisy had her own agenda. Her team was passing out fliers called, "The Proof is in the Pudding." The fliers had pictures of Malachai and Donlynne in a compromising position. At the same time the school television station was being hijacked and a segment of Donlynne and Arnie kissing and doing so much more appeared on the screen. I had a sense of déjà vu as I felt like I was on the set of one of my old videos. It was obvious that the moment they were sharing was intimate and that neither one of them knew or were aware that they were being recorded. I could see all eyes in Arnie's direction as the drink he was sipping on fell from his hand and splattered all over his suit and Donlynne's heels. Donlynne's face puffed up and she was wailing as she ran out of the reception. Some of her sisters were running after her. After the two minute clip was shown, a statement aired that said, "Let's keep it professional."

"She is such a hypocrite!" I was angry and slightly confrontational. Enough had been enough and I was beyond ticked off that nothing was being done to stop Daisy and her shenanigans.

"Lord, I hope she doesn't win," Mary said.

Elicia continued, "That was low. What Arnie and Donlynne do on their own time is their business. They shouldn't be outed like that."

"She must want someone to knock her out," Aaliyah jumped in, "even though I don't like ole' girl, that was still foul."

I was sure that neither one of us believed that Donlynne's and Arnie's having a premarital moment was appropriate or pleased God. Yet, I did feel that they had a right to deal with their sin in the privacy of their prayers to Him and to not have it broadcasted for others to make judgment. Donlynne came back into the banquet hall and she walked to the microphone. Her face showed where she was still fighting back tears. She gripped the microphone like a seasoned singer and she faced the audience.

"Okay, so I was caught and I guess the secret is out. Arnie is my man. To those of you who've known us and whom we tell our business to, then you've known that we've been together for over a year. So it's cool to know that someone would be so desperate to try to win that they would go as far as to follow us and publicize our most intimate moments. But you know what? I'd rather lose this race with some dignity and respect and to share my loss with a man who loves me as deeply as I love him than to win this crown in disgrace and embarrass North Carolina Technical University with my lack of class."

Donlynne put the microphone down and walked back to her and Arnie's campaign table. As she and Arnie embraced, everyone except Daisy's team stood up and clapped. It took a lot of guts for her to get up there and do that and for her not to give Daisy a beat down. She definitely showed the poise and class that her parents' brought her up with and showed why it was in her genes to go after this title. My respect for her grew at that point. Aaliyah even walked up to Donlynne and gave her a hug, which said a whole lot about how far their relationship had grown.

"I knew their secret would come out eventually," Elicia shook her head. "I hate that it came out like this."

"When did you find out?" Ezekiel asked. I hadn't even noticed him standing near us.

"I've known for a while now—I work for Arnie, or have y'all forgotten?"

A lot of people threw the fliers that Daisy's team passed out in the trash. Some guy in AGF picked up some drinks and poured them over the fliers in all the trash cans. Too bad that wasn't the only set of fliers that Daisy's team passed out. I knew the guy wished he was outside so he could set up a bonfire.

"I'm so glad I'm no longer part of that," Eric told me. I looked at the Elicia and Arnie placard he was wearing and smiled.

"Me too, brother," I shook his hand, "me too."

Go and Tell Mary and Martha - Election Day

*E*licia and I "skipped" all of our classes as did most of the candidates. We were in front of the Student Union passing out fliers and other goodies for the election. All of the candidates and campaign teams voted earlier in the day.

AGF had sponsored a reggae and go-go band to play all day. We watched as people danced all around and sang along with some of the songs. The group even played some of the popular gospel songs like "No Weapon" by Fred Hammond, "The Battle is Not Yours (It's the Lord's)" by Yolanda Adams and "God's Grace" by Trin-I-Tee 5-7. I was surprised at how nice the songs turned out.

Outside, Elicia and Mary were assigned to tables on the opposite ends of the Student Union. It didn't matter because our tables were the hot spots out of all the campaign tables. Mary and Elicia didn't let the distance stop them from hanging out either. They walked back and forth in their Sunday gear, wearing green suits and yellow tops. Arnisha, Lionel and Malachai were watching everything from their office at the top of the Student Union. They were also patrolling the borders to make sure no one entered the Student Union while promoting the candidates.

Donlynne's sorority sisters and campaign team were walking around like protestors promoting Donlynne for Miss NC Tech. They made a nice little circle in front of the Student Union. Then when the band started playing Jay-

Z's "Give it to Me," they started strolling. It was a hot watching them hold their fliers and do their stroll at the same time. Other members of Donlynne's team started picking up the fliers so that the girls can continue to do their thing. Arnie and his brothers starting strolling too, with Elicia, Aaliyah, Gabrielle and their sorority sisters following behind them. Ezekiel, Arnez and their fraternity followed and pretty soon, all the organizations were doing strolls and party hops. A lot of folks were grabbing their cameras and taking pictures and filming the event. I was on the sidelines with my non-dancing self, keeping up with the beat. I hadn't seen all the students strolling like that since right before the Homecoming step show.

Not to be outdone, AGF came out doing what they called "The Anti-Stroll." Basically they were making fun of the Greeks and throwing up their signs and messing up their call. Members of the school radio station made their way to the party and started playing songs from the seventies and eighties. I felt like I belonged doing the Cabbage Patch, the Running Man and the Electric Slide.

As serious as we were supposed to be trying to obtain votes and promoting our school policies, it was nice to have fun while promoting something as serious as SGA elections.

At six o'clock the polls were closed and all of the campaign teams set up shop in the Student Union.

Donlynne's mother and grandmother were in attendance. Arnie and his camp were sitting next to Donlynne's team while Donlynne and Arnie were offering support to one another. In one corner, Elicia and Mary and their teams were huddled together. Gabrielle was also chilling with us and having a good time. AGF and all their candidates had another corner on lock and some of the other candidates running for other offices had another corner. I looked for Daisy and her team but had not seen one member in sight.

"I am nervous," Elicia revealed to me. We were sitting together surrounded by others on our team.

"I got butterflies in my stomach," I revealed, "I haven't felt this nervous since I made my first video."

A bad reference but it was true.

"We put together a well-organized campaign. We were ready when the time came. All we have to do now is wait on God's will to be done." I was pleased to hear the confidence in Elicia's voice.

"Yes, win or lose it's God's will that will be done."

"I'm glad that Mary and I were able to keep our friendship intact."

"Me too."

Mrs. Edmonds and members of Shaw University's Student Government Association came through. Elicia hugged her brother tightly and they took a seat next to Elicia. Mary came over and gave everyone a hug, too. Daisy made a grand entrance to the Student Union. She had on a white dress with long white sleeves and a hat. No one was with her as she came over and sat where we were sitting. A lot of people were looking and pointing at us as we seemed to be hosting Daisy's return.

I approached her cautiously as I continued to look for other members of her campaign team. "Where are your people?" I asked, trying not to be rude, but curious.

Daisy looked at me and glared, "What people? I have no people."

"What about your team?" I was concerned because she had an army of eclectic people who supported her from the moment she announced that she was running to yesterday when she aired the video.

"If you want me to leave then I can leave," she yelled at me, "but I pay my tuition here just like everyone else does and if I want to sit here I will!" Daisy got up and stormed off. I questioned what I had said to provoke that response.

As she walked out of the Student Union, she bumped past Arnisha and Malachai as they came in.

"What's with her?" Malachai asked.

"Don't worry about her," Arnisha pulled the green and gold envelopes out of her bag, "let's do what we came here to do."

Malachai and Arnisha, along with members of the election team walked to the second floor of the Student Union. Overlooking the first floor, they both stood on the edge of the balcony. A janitor passed Arnisha the microphone.

"Greetings everyone," Arnisha commanded everyones attention, "we have the results of the class and SGA elections."

Malachai read the results of the class elections. Some of the students shouted and screamed and were filled with joy. Others were tense or disappointed in their results. We congratulated Ezekiel when it became official that he would lead our senior class as president. Malachai handed the mic to Arnisha, who announced the executive board officers.

"For SGA president, we have Gabrielle Carter," a large eruption of celebration filled the Student Union. Arnie came over and gave Gabrielle a hug and congratulated her. He went upstairs to the second floor and he took his spot with the outgoing executive board. Lionel was the only other person besides Donlynne who ran for office and he became our new SGA Treasurer. People clapped and congratulated Lionel for securing a spot for next year.

"That's all folks," Arnisha announced, "the elections for Miss NC Tech was so close, a winner has not been chosen."

A bunch of sighs filled the union. People started to get their stuff so they could leave and a bunch of people were congratulating winning candidates.

"Okay y'all, here it comes," Arnisha yelled as she saw members of the royal court arrive at the top of the balcony carrying a gold box with a big green bow tie wrapped around it. The court was dressed in the same outfits they wore for coronation. Malachai brought a chair and placed it behind Arnisha. Arnisha took a seat and she undid the ribbon on the box. She took out a crown and a sash and held them up. Miss North Carolina Technical University 2003-2004 was written neatly on the sash in green letters with a gold trim. She put the sash and crown back in the box.

"Our new Miss North Carolina Technical University is Mary Braxton!" Our team jumped and screamed for joy. Elicia and Mary were hugging each other tight with tears in each eye. Mary grabbed Elicia's arm and pulled her to the second floor to receive her crown. Arnez and I shook hands and many people within our two teams also shook hands and congratulated Mary's team for winning the campaign.

While Elicia and Mary were celebrating Mary's win, we could hear Donlynne sobbing. As I looked out to the attention Donlynne was demanding, I also noticed that Daisy was returning to the Student Union. Donlynne's mother and grandmother were comforting her and soon, Donlynne was crying on Arnie's shoulder. People clapped as Arnisha placed the sash on Mary's shoulder and the crown on her head. They hugged and Elicia and Mary hugged again. I looked at Monica's team and they were packing up their stuff and leaving without saying a word to anyone. This was a hard night for AGF because none of their candidates won any of the class or SGA offices they sought.

Donlynne made her way to the second floor to congratulate Mary. It was hard watching the hurt in her eyes, but at least she acknowledged her defeat. As for Daisy, she laid on the couch in one of the corners that had cleared. I felt a tap on my shoulder and was surprised to see Monica.

"Congratulations," Monica said.

"Thank you."

"I want to talk to you about Jesus. I need to get to know Him."

I reached for my bag and pulled my Bible out. In it, I had a bookmark that held the plan for salvation.

"Let me read this to you: First you have to admit that you are a sinner. The Bible says, 'Since all have sinned and fall short of the glory of God,' which can be found in Romans 3:23.

"Second, know that God has already provided for your salvation, 'For God so loved the world that he gave his only Son, so that everyone who believes in him may not perish but may have eternal life,' which is in John 3:16."

"So all I got to do is believe?" Monica asked. When I looked into her eyes, I remember my disbelief at how easy accepting Jesus seemed to be.

"Third, know that you cannot save yourself, 'He saved us, not because of any works of righteousness that we had done, but according to his mercy, through the water of rebirth and renewal by the Holy Spirit,' which is in Titus 3:5.

"Fourth, know that God's wrath abides on you, 'Whoever believes in the Son has eternal life; whoever disobeys the Son will not see life, but must endure God's wrath,' which is in John 3:36."

"See, I don't know if I'm going to be able to do this." Monica started to turn away. I reached out to grab her hand.

"We're not expected to be perfect." I reminded her. "Just ask Jesus Christ to save you, 'For everyone who calls on the name of the Lord shall be saved,' says Romans 10:13. Also, 'Believe on the Lord Jesus, and you will be saved, you and your household,' which is in Acts 16:31. You do believe don't you?"

With tears in her eyes, Monica confirmed. I shook my head because regardless of how short I fell, I still believed and I refused to believe that anyone would be able to take that from me.

"Then all you have to do is confess Jesus before men, 'If you confess with your lips that Jesus is Lord and believe in your heart that God raised him from the dead, you will be saved. For one believes with the heart and so is justified, and one confesses with the mouth and so is saved,' which is Romans 10:9 and 10.

"That is the plan of salvation, as it once was given to me by a good friend of mine. Do you accept?"

"Yes," Monica said.

"Welcome to the family," Mrs. Edmonds gave Monica a tight hug as she was holding her. Monica was crying hysterically and jumping up and down. Mary and Elicia ran downstairs to see the commotion.

"Thank you Jesus! Thank you for saving me," Monica was yelling loudly. Some of the people who were Christian were holding hands and hugging Monica as she began to start her journey with Jesus.

When I looked back at Daisy, something told me something wasn't right. I walked over to where she was laying. I nudged her on her shoulder and she still didn't move. Arnez reached over me and checked her pulse.

"Daisy, you okay! Daisy!"

Upon no response, Arnez directed someone to call 911. He tried to perform CPR on her to get her breathing. Ezekiel and I kept the crowd from getting close to them. The campus police and emergency crews took Daisy out of the Student Union and afterwards, the crowd dispersed.

Take Me to the Water - The Day After

By nine the next morning all the campaign fliers were down and school was almost back to normal. There was no word on Daisy's condition yet. Elicia's sorority had thrown a private dinner to celebrate Gabrielle's and Mary's win. We went to Ruby Tuesday on Wendover Avenue. The gathering was by invitation only and I had to make sure I had mine before I left.

When I got to Ruby Tuesday, I gave my invitation to one of the chapter members who escorted us to the room that we were in. When I walked in, Elicia gave me a big hug and escorted me to my seat. Gabrielle sat next to me as other guests sat down.

"Thanks for looking out for my girl," Gabrielle said.

"No problem, I always look out for Elicia."

"Well, I would like for you to be my Chief of Staff. I like how you handled business and have made a complete change in your life. You could be an example for others and we need more strong black males to serve as leaders on this campus. Plus, the fact that you are Christian doesn't hurt."

"Thanks—but what about Aaliyah and Elicia?" I was surprised because usually, the Chief of Staff appointment went to the campaign manager or a campaign staff person who worked hard to ensure the president's win. The pending appointment was totally unexpected.

"You know that Elicia will be working as Mary's assistant and will be helping Lionel get adjusted in his new position as treasurer. Aaliyah will have her hands full as chapter president and she will have a lot to do with our new members, Arnez will be taking over NAACP next school year, so that leaves you. You deserve it."

"In that case, I accept," Gabrielle and I hugged. Elicia came to sit next to me and I gave her a hug.

"How are you feeling?" I asked. I wanted her to be real with me.

"I'm blessed. I woke up this morning and I realized God's will is being done. As bad as I wanted it, it wasn't meant for me to be Miss North Carolina Technical University, and you know what, I'm okay with that."

"I just wanted to be sure."

"I did want to thank you again, for helping me."

"No problem baby girl, not at all."

We ordered our meal and ate and continued the celebration. One lesson I learned in this is that God sometimes uses you to fulfill a task or a journey for Him to put you in position to receive something bigger and better. Elicia's running wasn't for her to win but for others to see the Christ in her. From her campaign choices to how she did everything in her campaign that she promised, I prayed that everyone appreciate the example of God's mercy and grace that was beg shown through her.

Fall 2003

Soon and Very Soon - A Coronation

Alot has changed since Elicia ran for Miss North Carolina Technical University.

As it turned out, Donlynne was able to become SGA Public Relations Manager. Her family will get two more opportunities in five years to pursue a fourth generation Miss NC Tech when Donlynne's younger sisters are eligible to run. Her fiancé, Arnie became the president of the Council of Presidents, one of the most powerful organizations on campus that was only open to presidents of various clubs and organizations on campus and he was also appointed president of our school's Toastmasters chapter. Monica became a dedicated member of Women in the Spirit, a ministry group for women on campus. She still participated in some of the AGF activities, but she was no longer a prominent member.

As suspected, Daisy did try to commit suicide. I guess if I had been paying attention, I would have noticed that the signs were there that she needed help. The way that she tried to put everyone's business out and the way she tried to present herself in a bold and daring personality when she really was a calm person. She drew attention to herself so that she could be seen and paraded in front of other students and in the end, she got her reward. She took the rest of the semester off and planned to finish her studies under a special agreement with Tulane University.

Remember Keisha? How about that girl joined Elicia's sorority with Arnisha. That had to be the best kept secret since the mystery surrounding what was really in the pot pies the school loved to serve. Everyone and their mama was trying to get to their coming out show.

Elicia took her loss to Mary well. Of course, she was a little disappointed as I was to learn that she would not be Miss NC Tech but over the summer, we had plenty of time to get over that. She would be Mary's first attendant, assistant treasurer for another year and serve as the first second term president of Elite, Inc and president of Women in the Spirit. Personally, I didn't think the organization could have chosen a better woman to represent them on the campus.

We spent most of our summer at NC Tech participating in student orientation activities and giving tours of the campus. We also got to hang out with the Executive Board at A&T and we're even planning on doing some events together for this coming school year. In my opinion, I think that the three HBCUs in Greensboro could do more to work together and promote unity amongst our schools instead of being divisive. I think the divisive spirit raises pandemonium only because we as a people allow its ways to dictate and control our lives. There's nothing wrong with having pride in your school but don't take it to a point to where you put others down because they don't attend your school. A little competition is fun but some people just take it entirely too far.

Malachai completed his twelve-step program for sex addiction and went head on into politics working as an assistant to one of the state senators. He did a lot of traveling between Greensboro, Charlotte and Raleigh. He invited me to come to his grandparents' house in Clemmons to watch him burn his porno collection in their backyard. Now had this been a year and some change ago, I would have been highly offended that he burned my videos, but now, I felt like I was being redeemed for my past deeds. It's always good to get that reaffirmation that you are headed in the right direction and for me, if I didn't need any other confirmation I knew this one was it.

***

The fall semester was off to a great start. Working in student government, we spent weeks coming up with a theme for Homecoming that would top the previous years' shows. The goal was to reflect on the accomplishments of the past while showing the leadership taking NC Tech in a new direction. Once again, I had been drafted to participate in coronation, except this time it wasn't at the last minute.

We were lined up outside of the auditorium and we watched as some of the top designers from all over the country were coming in to take part of the festivities. Everyone was excited because nowhere in NC Tech's history has there ever been a coronation put on like this. The black and white limousines that were bringing sponsors and other guests continued to arrive and drop people off. When I looked to my left, I could see the crowd of students waiting to get into the event.

As we walked in, Kirk Franklin and God's Property were encouraging everyone to "Stomp." Watching the people dance and sing on their way in the auditorium was hilarious. Some of the people were actually trying to imitate the people in the video. I knew the vibe in the atmosphere. This coronation was definitely going to be like none other and very hard to top.

"What's up NC Tech!" Malachai roared as he came out from behind the curtains. "Today, we not only welcome you to the coronation, but we also debut the spring and summer collection of our talented and gifted 2003 – 2004 Miss North Carolina Technical University, Mary Braxton."

The crowd rose in an uproar. They still could not believe that they were going to be treated to a first class fashion show. It was very hard to convince the modeling troupes to cancel their fashion show but once they found out what Mary had in store, they had no choice but to oblige. What other theme did anyone expect Mary to come up with but do a top rate fashion show? This year, the modeling troupes were able to sponsor the national touring of the latest Tyler Perry play for a special one-day performance in place of their fashion show. The play bought a large number of people to the Greensboro Coliseum and ended up being one of our most profitable events our Student Government Association put on in a while.

"It is good that God is in the house," Malachai announced once the crowd wound down. "In a tribute to her inspiration and her creativity, the clubs and organizations around campus will be showcasing Mary's various designs and styles."

The social clubs came out first wearing spring gear. The men were rocking various polo's and short sleeve shirts with either shorts or slacks. The women came out wearing T-Shirts that had slogans like "Free Mary" and "It's Not Over." The academic societies were next and they were wearing various lounge wear. I noticed that more people at NC Tech were comfortable wearing these pajama pants to and from class and all over the place. At first I thought this was a NC Tech thing but when I went to A&T and Bennett, I noticed the same thing. Okay, maybe this was a new fad. The civic organizations were next and they modeled summer wear to go to the beach or to hang out at the park. The sororities and the fraternities were wearing the swimwear and I have to say, I could see myself wearing some of the swimwear they had modeled. I would probably even rock some of the Speedos.

At any rate, our turn came and the new executive board members were wearing tailored clothes to go to evening events and to church. The crowd was hype and as true to what Mary said at the pageant, I was wearing a black suit with a silver tie and a Kangol. They even had Youtube video clips playing on monitors throughout the school in which people were allowed to see me get dressed for today's event. The hats that Mary made were nice—they should have been in the *Crowns* book that was published a few years ago by a few local authors and photographers. Maybe we could get in touch with those guys and have them do a part two.

"Now, for the woman of the hour," Malachai announced after all the organization representatives ripped the runway and took their seats on first ten rows in the coliseum, "she is a senior, Fashion Design and Business Education Major from College Park, Georgia. She is also the designer and CEO of Miriam and Mary Designs. Please welcome our 2003-2004 Miss North Carolina Technical University, Mary Braxton!"

As Mary's segment came on, Faith Evans surprised everyone and came out singing her hit single, "Burnin'." Another shock was that Mary was singing the song with Faith. They looked nice bringing back those skorts that people used to wear. Faith had on this crème hat with a matching crème and black checkered shirt. Her red hair was pulled back and her hat was tilted to where you couldn't see her face, kind of like Carmen Sandiego. Mary, on the other hand had her hair cut like Missy Elliot did on her album cover. Everyone was on their feet as the two ladies continued to sing. When the song was over, the ladies left and then Mary came out a second later wearing a nice evening gown that she designed herself. It had sequins all over the place on the red dress. She had on long gloves and some high heels to match. She took a seat on her throne and the crowd followed suit.

Arnisha came in riding a light blue and silver motorcycle to the stage. She took her helmet off and shook her hair loose and we could see the crown still attached to her head. She readjusted her crown in the motorcycle's mirror and then walked to the back where she unfastened a box. She was wearing a motorcycle bodysuit that had the Miriam and Mary Designs logo on the front and throughout the side. I had forgotten that Arnisha liked to ride motorcycles as we didn't see her on the bike at all while she was reigning as Miss NC Tech. Arnisha walked with the box to the thrown and she kneeled before Mary.

"Girl, let me tell you, this suit is phat! I almost didn't make it here because I had to fight the men off who were chasing me," Arnisha said as everyone let out a small laugh at her comment. Mary got up and she took the crown out of the box. Arnisha helped put it on her head and the crowd clapped again. I was proud of her.

"I want to thank everyone who voted for me and just voted period," Mary spoke through the tears. There was clapping and when it died down, Mary continued. "This is for my ladies. Regardless of whether you have the title or not, you have to represent North Carolina Technical University in your words and in your actions. You can't just get up in the morning and go to your business class in pajamas or your evening class in your club gear. How you present yourself when you walk out of that door in the morning is how people are going to remember you. If you say you're saved, people are going to look for you to represent that cross whether you wear it or not." More claps filled the room. "You have to stay on your game and you can stay on your game. Don't let temptation lead you to a game you don't have any business playing. I want to thank my parents, Mr. & Mrs. Antonio Braxton, my fellow executive board members and a very special friend, Elicia

Edmonds. Girl, we couldn't have planned this coronation without you."

Elicia stood up and took a bow. After Mary finished her acknowledgements, Faith Evans came back and sang "Holy, Holy, Holy" and everyone was feeling it. That song has always been one of my favorite gospel numbers and to hear her put her spin on it was nice indeed. You could tell Faith had those gospel roots as she began to hit those various notes in the song.

After coronation was over with, we went to the ballroom for another reception. Ezekiel and I were hanging out and talking to some other people in our class. This plus-sized woman bumped into me and stepped on my toe.

"My bad," she said. "I meant to say excuse me."

She was beautiful. She had a full face with light brown, chocolate themed makeup and short, bouncy curls that seemed to bloom from her crown. She reminded me a little of Kelly Price, except a little slimmer.

"You're fine sweetie, you're fine."

I watched as the woman walked away. She smiled when she looked back and seen that I was still looking in her direction.

"I think she likes you Donte," Ezekiel teased.

"Be quiet."

We went back and joined the executive board and the rest of the guests at the festivities. I looked for her in the crowd but I didn't see her anymore. Maybe I'll see her again, and when I do, I'll remember to ask for her name.

When I got back to my apartment, Malachai and I had a small get together for the current executive board's families and friends. Malachai's family had come up here all the way from Phoenix to celebrate the homecoming festivities. I saw Malachai standing out the door way holding his son, Junior. Junior looked so much like his daddy that it wasn't even funny. He put Junior down and Junior ran out of the room.

"Junior's mama is in Nashville—it's hard going back and forth trying to visit him and getting him to come see me," Malachai revealed as he sat down at the table and ate a few Buffalo wings with ranch dressing from his plate. "As much as I love working for the senator, I'm thinking of moving to Nashville when he retires at the end of this term." As Malachai put the wing to his lips, I noticed the imprint on his finger from where his wedding band once was. That was odd because he *always* wore his band ever since he eloped with that lady whom had given birth to his son a few months ago. His speaking of Nashville reminded me of the last time I had been. I was hocking sales of my video right in the middle of 5th Avenue South near the Country Music Hall of Fame. Since I almost got arrested for loitering among other things, I hadn't been to Nashville since. At first, I'm not even going to lie, I didn't think I would have an audience in Nashville. Usually, the first impression you got was Elvis Presley, country music and being "The Buckle of the Bible Belt." Yet, I soon discovered that Nashville was so much more. There were a lot more Blacks than I thought there would be, even though I had family there. The city had listed as one of *Black Enterprises'* "Top 10 Cities for African Americans" for the past year. And with the burgeoning rap scene that was starting to grow in Memphis, it was just a matter of time that the music from the Mississippi River made it to the center of the state.

"That sounds interesting. It would be nice to be back in entertainment in a new city and working for the Lord. But I need to get some money together for me to go." That was all I had gotten to say before we heard a loud knock and then a cry at the door. I was about to walk out when I noticed a toddler sitting in a car seat at the door.

"What the—" I looked down and saw my fish lapel on my shirt and remembered that I wasn't supposed to cuss. I picked the toddler up from the seat and carried him to the couch. Malachai grabbed the car seat and the bag next to it and brought it in. "It's too cold for this mess!" I had almost slipped but in my mind, I had said what I had wanted to say and I immediately repented.

"Ooooh, a baby," one of the younger children gets up and runs from the table.

"We have a baby," the excitement grew as the little boy starts crying in my arms. I try to cradle and comfort him to ease his crying.

"Children sit down!" Malachai commanded as he took the bag and the car seat and placed it on the table. Attached to the bag was a blue note. I had undressed the little boy to inspect him for any bumps and bruises. I had wanted to get the phone so I could call the police but Malachai shook his head at me. Malachai got a look at the boy's face and replied, "Something about the boy looks familiar." Malachai opened the note and began to read:

Sup Donte,

I know you know who this is. It wasn't fun being asked to leave your bed in the middle of the night or the fact that you forgot my name. But that's okay though, I have forgiven you for that.

I remember when you had gotten into that big scandal a few years back with this chick telling everybody that you were her baby's father. So after a search, I had one of my home girls, Dana, pull up your files and match the baby's paternity with yours. I guess you got another reason to celebrate today because this is your son, Eugene. I know you are into the "Christian" thing which I think is crazy right about now, but on second thought, I know you can do more for Eugene than I can. I'm going to try to respect the fact that you got your Christian image to uphold and having said that, I know you will do the right thing. I'm not trying to follow Jesus right now, but I know that if you can forgive me for keeping this baby a secret from you all this time and not being woman enough to tell you about your son all the times I used to run into and run from you, this boy will be the young man he is destined to be.

My Early Christmas Present to You,

Eve

My mom was in shock and passed out. My younger brother reached into our mom's purse and pulled out some kind of medicine when her wallet fell out. I reached for it and grabbed it and I found our baby pictures. I looked at Eugene and then at the pictures of my brother and I when we were toddlers. I was confused and then I looked at Eugene. He did look like us when we were babies.

I got to thinking of the nightmare I used to have about Eve and I creating a baby and I thought back to my last night with her when I made my last video. I looked at the little boy again, who seemed to have calmed down and started laughing and giggling when I moved. I smiled, too, but I was beginning to wonder what would Jesus do?

About the Author

Over the years, Isaiah David Paul has written in a variety of genres and became a writing partner and ghostwriter for a few award-winning and best-selling authors. With his string of successes and renewed faith in God, Isaiah David Paul has finally decided to follow his calling to write under his own name. He has a business management degree from North Carolina Agricultural & Technical State University, a Masters of Entrepreneurship from Western Carolina University and a MAT-Elementary Education from the University of North Carolina at Greensboro. He is the author of over fifty titles under various pseudonyms and has contributed to the publication of nearly two hundred books. He lives a private life with his family in the Southeast United States.

Follow Isaiah David Paul on Social Media:

Official Website	IsaiahDavidPaul.com
Instagram	@IsaiahDavidPaul
TikTok	@IsaiahDavidPaul
Blue Sky	@IsaiahDavidPaul
Facebook	@IsaiahDavidPaul
Linktree	@IsaiahDavidPaul
X/Twitter	@IsaiahDavidPaul